SCREAMS

OF

LATE SPRING

A Rebel Joe™ Story

Dan Sanders

To Becky, my muse

CHAPTER 1

When the train whistle screamed, it frightened me worse than last time. My heart raced even harder than before too. The passenger car I was riding in was at the front of the train, and the sound really hurt my ears. The locomotive hollered, rumbled, and groaned as the train climbed up a hill. After a moment, I looked up at Leonard and noticed that he was smiling down at me.

"Sure is loud, ain't it?" he remarked.

"Yes, sir."

Leonard laughed, "Sittin' in the front seat of the first car of a loud train ain't the best way to ride the rails, now is it?"

Leonard was funny. I looked around the passenger car, which was almost full, but the other passengers didn't seem scared. The woman behind me was reading a book and holding a sleeping baby. Across the aisle, a man wearing a hat looked like he was asleep too. The train whistle didn't seem to bother the fat man and his fat wife nearby, either.

I turned back around and looked at Leonard. He was a porter for the railroad. Leonard had gotten his ukulele down and let me play it by myself. Pop had asked Leonard to watch me while he went to talk with someone in the rear of the train. "OK, young Russ, try to put all three chords together now," Leonard instructed.

"Yes, sir," I replied. I knew two of the chords already because Mom had taught them to me. She played piano. Last fall, Pop and I traveled to Cincinnati to see her perform in a big theater. Everyone clapped whenever she finished a song. Pop and I clapped too.

Mom had been teaching me how to play the ukulele, and she said I was getting better every day. And now, Leonard had just taught me a third chord, so I made sure not to forget it.

"Start with F, strum, strum, strum," Leonard said.

I sat up straight, put my fingers on the strings and frets, and started to strum.

"Good work, Russ. Now go to G seventh," he said.

G seventh was the chord Leonard had just taught me. I put my fingers in the right spots and played it fairly well. I had never played a chord with three fingers before. But I did it!

"OK, go to C seventh," Leonard requested.

I knew that chord. It was the easiest one to play, and I liked the way it sounded. I moved my finger to the first fret of the first string and strummed three more times.

"Well done, young Russ! Now, play it again."

After I played the three measures again, Leonard clapped for me then shook my hand. I had played a waltz. Mom had taught me how to count out a waltz: One, two, three. One, two, three. One, two, three. And now I'd just played a three-chord waltz. I couldn't wait to show Mom when Pop and I got home!

"Excellent playing, young Russ! Excellent playing!" Leonard praised. "You must be thirteen or fourteen years old by now, ain't ya?"

"Thank you, sir," I said. "I'm ten," I added with a laugh.

"Coulda fooled me," Leonard said with a wide grin.

Ten years old. Two digits, I thought to myself. Ten was a big deal. It was an entire decimal point. Pop said that being ten meant having to act like a young man instead of a little boy.

Leonard reached for the ukulele. "Now, young Russ, I hafta get some work done, or they'll throw me off this train fo' sure." I knew he was just joking. Leonard gently put his uke back in its case and stashed it in the closet. "I'll come check on you in a while, and we can play again."

"Thank you, sir. That would be nice."

Leonard tipped his cap to me then walked forward and began stacking some coffee cups. I'd been a little sad when Pop left me by myself up at the front of the train, but Leonard had cheered me up.

I peered through the window and noticed that it was still dark outside. I could see the track below us whenever we passed a lamp, but mostly it was too dark to see anything. The train was traveling southwest, so I wouldn't see the sun come up unless I was at the back of the train. I checked the pocket watch Pop had given me. It was a railman's watch, just like his. I had memorized the sunrise and sunset times for the day, so I knew the sun would be coming up in a few minutes.

Pop worked for the railroad: the B & O . . . this railroad . . . his railroad . . . my railroad. Pop didn't even need a ticket to ride the train; he just got on whenever and wherever he wanted. I also got to ride for free when I was with him. Everybody knew Pop and said hello to him, especially this morning when we got to the depot. I was eager to get on the train, but Pop had to talk with about a million people. And each one of them told me I looked just like him.

When the train whistle screamed again, my heart leaped. I could feel it pounding in my chest. Finally, after a while, it went back to normal. It used to worry me when I was younger, so I told Mom about it. But she made me go to the doctor, and the doctor said I had to stay in bed for a week. He asked me if I felt muddled. I didn't know what that meant, so I told him I did. From then on, I called it being muddled, and I hated it.

I couldn't go outside or do anything for a whole

week. It was the worst week of my entire life.

After the week was over, I just told Mom that my heart had stopped racing. She was so happy and relieved to hear that, she must've hugged me a hundred times. When she took me back to the doctor, I told him the same thing, and I was allowed to play outside again. After a while, Mom just quit asking me about it. My heart still beats really fast sometimes. When I feel it coming on, I get a little dizzy. I just don't tell Mom . . . or Pop. I don't tell nobody, just myself.

I looked out the window and saw the first light of the morning, as some dark blue sky blended in with the pitch black. I glanced down and saw the ground rushing by us. Just then, I noticed that the man beside me and the baby behind me were both awake. The baby appeared to be a girl, and she was a little fussy. She reminded me of my sister, Betty, back when she was a baby. I used to do a trick to make Baby Betty laugh. I peeked over the seat at the girl and smiled. She stared back at me with big, blue eyes. I put my finger in my mouth, puffed up my cheeks, and quickly pulled out my finger. When I did that, it made a loud *pop* sound, which made the baby giggle. Her mother glanced up at me and smiled. I already missed Betty and Mom a little, but I didn't want Pop to know.

Pop! I made the sound again, and the baby laughed. Pop does it to say "hello" to me. Pop and I were the only two people I knew who could make that sound. None of my friends could do it.

Earlier, Pop had gone to the rear of the train.

He was probably out on the vestibule smoking a cigar watching the sun come up. Mom said Pop's cigars smelled like a gypsy's ass. Pop told her that wasn't a very ladylike thing to say. Then Mom told him it wasn't a nice thing for a lady to smell. Mom always managed to get in the last word with Pop.

Sometimes, Pop didn't come home for days. I missed him when he was gone, but he would always give me a big hug when he got home. This time I got to go on the train with him. I had hoped it would be a lot of fun, but I hadn't seen very much of Pop so far. I was feeling a bit lonely, so I decided to go look for him.

As I walked slowly down the aisle to the back of the car, I spied on all the passengers. I liked people watching. Pop did too. I passed people who were sleeping, so I stayed as quiet as I could. Pop had told me that was the polite thing to do. When I got to the back of the passenger car, I waved to Peter. Peter was a porter like Leonard, but he looked a bit older. He gave me a wide smile and said, "You're Pop's boy, aren't ya?"

"Yes, sir," I replied.

"Pop's a good man. We all love him 'round here," Peter said. Then he turned around and went back to work. I loved Pop too. I figured he was the smartest man in Indiana—most likely Kentucky too. He kept all the trains running on time for the railroad. Everybody said so.

I've always wondered why everyone called my father Pop. I called him Pop because a lot of kids called their fathers that—which makes sense. But everyone who knew my father also called him Pop. Mom and Betty called him Papa, which isn't much different. But whenever we took the train anywhere, everyone wanted to shake hands with my father, and they all called him Pop. I guessed it was just his nickname.

At the back of the passenger car, I pulled down on the door handle. It was heavy, but I was able to get it open and step into the vestibule—the section of the train that connected the cars. I gazed through the big open window on the side and then stuck out my head. The wind blew in my face and tousled my hair as I breathed in the warm air. Pop said this was going to be one of the hottest days of the summer.

The acrid-smelling smoke billowing above the locomotive made my eyes water a bit. Pop said some people didn't like the smell of a train engine, but he did—so I did too. I liked all the same things as Pop. Sometimes, Pop and I would wave to all the people the train passed, and they would wave back. It was my favorite thing to do on the train during a ride. But it was still too early and too dark to see anyone outside, so there was no one to wave to.

Pop had taken me to the picture show the week before. He loved going to the movies because there was no such thing when he was a boy. Betty was still too young, so Pop and I would go to the movies alone, which was fine by me because he bought me "sodee" pop and candy. Pop would puff on his cigar and laugh during the show, even during scary parts. Pop had the loudest belly laugh I'd ever heard.

In the show we'd recently seen, a good cowboy

chased a bad cowboy all through a train, up the ladder, and then onto the roof. While the train was chugging swiftly down the track, the two cowboys ran across the train's roof and jumped from car to car. Pop called them train walkers. He laughed during the chase scene, but I was a little scared, so I covered my eyes a bit. When the good guy shot the bad guy, the bad guy fell off the train. Then the good guy had to duck and lay flat as the train steamed into a tunnel. Since seeing that movie, I'd secretly been thinking about becoming a train walker—which seemed pretty easy to me—but I didn't tell Mom or Pop.

Big Tunnel was the only tunnel on this stretch of the railroad. No one could lie down and make it through that tunnel, though—they'd get squashed. Pop told me that passenger cars expand in the summertime, so if a train went too slow through a tunnel like that, a hot passenger car could get stuck until it cooled down, and that could cause a crash. I asked him what he would do if that happened. Pop chuckled and said he'd probably have to find another job. I wondered if Pop was pulling my leg.

There used to be a Little Tunnel too, but they cut off the top of the hill, and now it's a gorge. I could picture in my head where each tunnel was located along the route. Whenever Pop was away, I would study his maps over and over again until I had memorized some of them. When Pop would get home, he'd test me to see if I knew all the stops. If I missed one, he would say "WRONG!" and laugh and wrestle with me. Pop's a funny guy.

I had ridden this stretch of the railroad my

whole life. I had ridden it as far east as Cincinnati and as far west as St. Louis, even though we had to get on a different train to go across the Mississippi. Pop said some passengers rode this stretch as they traveled across the country. I often wondered what it would be like to ride the rails all the way to the West Coast. I wondered what the mountains looked like . . . and the ocean. I'd never seen an ocean before except in pictures.

On this particular day, Pop and I were just taking the train to Mitchell, so it was going to be a pretty short trip. My cousin Birdy—who was a year older than me—lived in Mitchell, and I couldn't wait to see him. I was smarter than Birdy, and he was bigger than me, but he was my best friend in the whole world. Everybody liked Birdy because he was always smiling and having a good time. Pop and his brother, Uncle Walt—that's Birdy's dad—were also best friends, so I figured they'd be happy to see each other too.

Pop and I left very early this particular morning, so we took the daily 97, which is a second-class train. Most of the time our family traveled to Mitchell on the daily 67—a first-class train. Mom loved the daily 67 because it was so luxurious. Mom would speak to me very dramatically in French, which would make me laugh. But if she talked to me in German, that meant she was mad at me. On the first-class trains, the seats were soft and new. The porters would bring me sodee pop with ice, and everyone treated me like I was a young man and called me sir. Whenever we traveled on board the 67, people would ask Mom to play the piano. Pop said Mom used to play the piano on the trains sometimes when she was younger. I always loved to watch her play.

I studied the window on the vestibule for

a moment, watching the trees speed past outside. Then, without even thinking, I climbed into the open window, held on to the railing above, and then leaned out over the side of the train as far as I could. As the wind rushed past me, I kind of wished the train would go faster. I knew I would never be able to do this if Mom or Pop were around. Mom would yell at me, and Pop might give me a skinning, even though he never had before. Even so, I often did stunts on trains that Mom and Pop wouldn't allow. And I kept it a secret from everyone except Birdy because I told him everything. He laughed and said he wouldn't show up to my funeral if I died. *What does Birdy know, anyway?* I thought.

After a few moments, I climbed back in through the window then made my way over to the other side of the vestibule, wondering if I could walk on top of the train. I wanted to climb up and see what the top of the passenger car looked like so I could tell if train walking would be easy or not. *I'll just scout it out*, I thought to myself.

Like I'd done on the other side, I crawled into the window and swung out away from the train. This time, I noticed a ladder running up the side of the car. The rungs weren't large, but I figured my feet would fit. As I contemplated my next move, I swung back in through the window. As I hopped down, I froze when I noticed a man watching me. I hadn't heard him come through the door. He was the biggest man I'd ever seen, a real-life giant. *Uh-oh . . . I'm in trouble now.*

CHAPTER 2

Friday, June 13, 1924, 5:39 a.m.

Vallonia, Indiana

"**W**hatcha tryin' t'do, kid, get yuhself killed?" the Giant growled. He appeared to be the kind of man who didn't like kids.

I got muddled; I couldn't move or speak. I felt my pulse pound faster than a piston. The Giant had black, slicked-back hair and wore a pinstripe suit and tie, just like Pop, but he was much larger than Pop, and his hands were enormous. He also wore a bowler hat and rings on his fingers. I wondered how he got the rings on and off with his sausage-like digits. He had the meanest eyes I'd ever seen, and they seemed to pierce my soul. I knew in an instant that he was a killer, and I was in big trouble, so I tried to stay calm.

"What's da madder? Cat got yer tongue?" he said. He gave me a menacing look as he stared down at me. "What are ya, a simp? Is that it, boy? Are ya a damn simp?"

I wanted to say that I wasn't, but I didn't say a word. Pop always said to think before I spoke, and if I didn't have anything smart to say, then I shouldn't say anything at all because it would make things worse. As I quickly glanced at the Giant, I noticed that on the left side of his belt and inside his open

11

jacket, he had a government Colt pistol in a holster. *He's left-handed*, I thought. I had learned that when Pop read me Sherlock Holmes. The sight of the gun terrified me.

"Simps who climb on da train get killed. Ya understand me, boy? How old are ya?" he barked. He glared down at me for a long time.

Finally, I felt that I had to say something so he'd leave me alone. "Ten, sir," I finally whispered.

The Giant looked around and then returned his gaze to me. "Ya don't look ten. Now, go back to yer seat and stay dare, ya hear?" he ordered, poking his index finger into my chest. It felt like someone had punched me. "Stay in dat seat, ya hear me, boy?"

"Yes, sir," I responded.

In my eyes, the Giant was the scariest man in the world, so I stood completely still. After a while, the Giant looked around again, glared at me for what seemed like forever, and then opened the door to the passenger car. He turned and gave me one last angry stare before closing the door, which made a crashing noise when it shut.

When I realized I was shaking and on the brink of tears, I took a deep breath. Until then, I hadn't even noticed that I'd been holding my breath. I inhaled deeply, walked over to the window, and gazed out. The sun was beginning to rise, so I could see the trees outside. The Giant had moved toward the front of the train, so I made my way toward the rear, trying not to attract attention.

The next car was more crowded than the one I'd been sitting in, so most of the seats were taken. Toward the front of the car, I noticed a couple of families, a soldier, a peculiar old lady, and an old man reading the *Seymour Tribune*. But I didn't see Pop, so I decided to check the next car. As I meandered down the aisle, I didn't look at anybody; I just stared at my shoes.

"Hi!" said a lanky redheaded kid. He came out of nowhere and startled me a bit.

"I'm Armstead, but people call me Army." He stuck out his hand. I shook it and made eye contact like Pop had taught me.

Army was a little taller than me, and I could tell just by looking at him that he didn't live in town, he lived out in the country for sure. He seemed older than me, but not by much, and he had freckles all over his face and arms. One of the straps on his large denim overalls had been broken and sewn back on crooked, which made me think his mom couldn't sew very well. And his boots were dirty. I wondered if his dad hadn't taught him how to shine them like Pop had taught me. I could shine my boots better than any kid my age. I wanted to tell the red-haired bumpkin he could shine his, too, if he just practiced.

I spied his family and noticed that he had four sisters! *Poor kid*, I thought. I didn't see his dad anywhere, though. Maybe he'd run away when he learned he had four daughters. "What's your name?" Army asked.

"I'm Johnny," I lied. I didn't know why.

"You wanna play checkers?" Army asked. He pointed to his checkerboard, but I was looking at the uneaten apple in his left hand. It was easy to feel bad for him because he was probably bored stiff traveling with his mom and four sisters, but I really didn't want to play checkers. I wanted something to eat. Pop had made us breakfast before we left, but he wasn't a very good cook. All I got was some burnt toast, which Pop said would put hair on my chest. Pop was full of it sometimes. I was starving, and Army's apple looked good.

"Is that your checkerboard?" I asked.

"Yeah. . . . You know how to play?"

"I'm just learning," I fibbed. "Can you show me?" I knew how to play, I just needed him to turn around so I could swipe his apple. I knew it was wrong, and I felt sorry for him, but I was hungrier than I'd ever been. I'd never lift an apple from Birdy or my sister, Betty, but I didn't know this kid from Adam. Plus, I'd never see him again. Still, I knew it was wrong. Pop had said on more than one occasion that if people are nice to you, you should be nice to them.

Even so, I decided to steal his apple, which gave me butterflies in my stomach. I hoped he wouldn't catch me. I knew I'd have to be quick about it. Army put the apple down on the armrest and turned to pick up the checkerboard. I swiped his apple with my left hand and put it in my pants pocket.

As he slowly turned back around, checkerboard in hand, he did a masterful job of keeping the pieces in place while the train swayed, rattled, and rolled. I was impressed.

"Wow, that's a great checkerboard!" I exclaimed with mock enthusiasm.

"So, Johnny, you wanna play?" he asked, putting the checkerboard down.

"Oh boy, do I!" I replied with a smile.

Army smiled back and bounced up and down a little with eager anticipation. Birdy did that too when he got excited.

"But first I have to go check with my father," I replied casually. "I'll be right back." I started walking down the aisle toward the rear of the train, but then Army started following me. *I bet he doesn't follow instructions in school—if he even goes to school*, I thought. I pretended not to notice, but I wasn't happy about him following me.

Lucky for me, the shrill sound of Army's mother's voice broke through the noise of the passenger car, "Armstead, get back here and sit down! I won't tell you again!" She looked bigger than a stonecutter and just as mean. I guess Army figured he'd best mind his mama, so he stopped following me. Again, I just kept walking. When I reached the door, I opened it, stepped into the vestibule, and took a deep breath.

I needed to put some distance between me and the redheaded kid so I could eat his apple. Plus, I still

15

needed to get as far away from the Giant as I possibly could. I made my way into the next passenger car and inspected it. It was even more crowded than the one Army and his family were stuck in. I didn't see Pop there, either. I walked down the aisle looking for an empty seat, but there were none, so I kept moving.

Once I made it to the next vestibule, my stomach grumbled. I was sure I was the hungriest kid in the world, and I couldn't stop myself, so I tore into Army's apple. It was delicious! I devoured it quickly and threw the core off the train. "Jack," I remarked, thinking of the country bumpkin. In Pop's mystery novels, Sherlock Holmes referred to the people who got taken as marks. But Birdy, Pop, and Uncle Walt called them jacks, so I called them jacks too. I had taken Army, so that made him a jack. Soon, I realized I wasn't that sorry I took his apple. I figured if there had to be a jack, it wasn't ever going to be me.

I stood in the vestibule for a bit, and then I looked out the window and, once again, noticed a metal bar running alongside it. The ladder in front of me led to the roof. I contemplated climbing the ladder to see what the top of this passenger car looked like. But then I remembered my run-in with the Giant and realized that I didn't want him to catch me again. *I'd be a goner, for sure*, I thought. *But, then again, what are the chances that he'll come back this way?*

I heaved myself out the window and grabbed onto the bar. The wind whipped at my body as the train barreled forward. I counted to myself, *one, two, three*, and then swung my foot over to the top of the bottom rung of the ladder. But I missed and started to slip. I tried once more, but my foot slipped again.

At this point, both my feet were dangling below the vestibule as I struggled to hang onto the bar. I tried to kick my foot back up a couple of times, but I couldn't get it to reach the first rung of the ladder or the window of the vestibule. I almost cried as I started to panic.

In my frenzied state, I remembered a story Pop had told me once about a man who had been hit by a train and had both his legs ripped clean off. I imagined looking down at my legs and seeing them cut off. In my mind, they looked like big hams with the bone still in them. Thinking like that only frightened me more, and I wasn't sure how much longer I could hold on. "Think!" I heard Pop say in my head. "Think!"

As I tried to figure out what to do, I noticed a rail in between the door and ladder—I just wasn't sure I could reach it. I tried as hard as I could and grabbed ahold of the rail, causing my whole body to swing forward. Keeping one hand on the rail and the other on the ladder. *Whew . . .* , I thought. *Now I have some leverage.* At that point, I was able to lift myself up a bit—just enough that I could place my left foot square on the bottom rung, followed soon by my other foot. Now that I was out of danger, I exhaled deeply.

When the train's whistle blew, it didn't scare me this time. Instead, I caught my breath and stayed where I was for a moment as the trees flew by in a blackish-green blur. As I thought about how to get my feet on the next rung, I started reconsidering my desire to be a train walker. I figured if I could get out of this jam, I'd find a seat in a passenger car, and no one would ever need to know about this incident.

But then again, I could climb up, put my feet on the next rung, and see what the roof of the passenger car looked like. The bad kid inside me prodded the good young man to keep climbing. I hated the bad kid inside me sometimes because he often got me in trouble, but I decided to keep going anyway. Suddenly, the train lurched to the right and my feet slipped off the bottom rung. I held on with both hands as tight as I could, and when the train jerked back, my body slammed into the side of the car. In the process, I almost lost my grip with my left hand for just a second and almost fell beneath the train. Somehow, I managed to hang on and lock my left foot in between the ladder and the train. Then I kicked my other foot back onto the bottom rung. When I felt the car start to sway again, I locked both my feet around the bottom rung. So, even though the train tottered back and forth, I stayed still.

At that point, I decided I'd come too far not to see the roof of the train, so I said to myself, "You can do this, Russ." Then I pulled myself up one rung at a time until I reached the top. It was actually easier than I thought it would be. Although the train rocked back and forth, I managed to keep my balance and finally made it to the roof.

CHAPTER 3
Friday, June 13, 1924, 6:26 a.m.
Fort Ritner, Indiana

Lying on top of the train, I breathed in the smoky air. From my perch high above, I could feel the vibrations from the tracks below. Gazing down at the big steel wheels rolling below me, I started to shake as I, once again, envisioned my legs being torn off. I tried not to think about it and put it out of my mind as best I could.

I willed myself not to look down and, instead, inspected the roof of the passenger car. I figured I could walk on it if I wanted to, or I could crawl along it on my hands and knees. However, I decided then and there that I didn't want to be a train walker, so I stayed right where I was.

Even though the climb to the roof of the train was terrifying, the magnificent view made it all worthwhile. Steam and smoke poured out of the locomotive as it chugged along. And as the breeze caressed my face and billowed through my hair, I could see all the passenger cars in front of and behind me. I scanned the woods and rolling hills laid out on either side of the tracks and allowed myself a huge grin as I breathed a sigh of relief. *Maybe I should climb up here every time I take this route?*

While I was on the roof of the passenger car, the train steamed its way toward Fort Ritner. It wouldn't stop unless a priority daily was coming from the other direction, and I knew from Pop's timetables that none were coming this way.

Fort Ritner was a small town, but people were milling about and looking at the train. Usually, whenever we'd go through towns like this, I'd wave to people, and they'd wave back and smile. But this time, I didn't wave; I was too afraid to let go of the railing along the roof.

The train slowed down as we passed through Fort Ritner, and I noticed something kind of strange. Instead of people waving at passengers on the train, they were pointing at the train, and some children were clapping their hands. That seemed odd. When I heard a man say something about a kid on top of the train, I realized they were all pointing at me. I was the kid on top of the train!

"Dang it!" I said to no one but myself. I hadn't thought my plan through enough to consider what would happen if anyone saw me on the roof of the train. *I'll have to plan better next time.* I knew I'd get into a lot of trouble if I got caught. Pop might skin me. Or worse, he'd tell me he was disappointed in me.

When the train whistle blew three times, I decided it was time to get back into the train—and fast. Three whistles meant a tunnel was coming. I had forgotten about the Big Tunnel, which actually wasn't all that big. In fact, it had an exceedingly small clearance on top. I knew I would get squished for sure if I stayed up here any longer.

As the train continued to sway, I carefully made my way back to the ladder where I dropped down hand over hand before swinging my feet back into the window of the vestibule. It was much easier getting down, but I figured I'd be better at the climbing up part next time. I grabbed the bar above me, lifted my butt off the window, and hopped back into the vestibule, landing on my feet like a professional tumbler.

The first thing I noticed inside the vestibule was the Giant glaring at me. He looked even meaner than before. I stood there frozen, just staring down at the floor. I tried to look for a way out, but there wasn't one. The Giant had me trapped, and I didn't want to face him.

I need to find Pop, I thought. *Everyone knows Pop.* But I wasn't going anywhere with the Giant blocking my way. I thought quick and sputtered, "I'm Pop's boy." I smiled at the Giant, but he continued to scowl at me.

"Pahp cain't help ya now, ya damn simp," he snarled. Then he pulled back the left side of his jacket, where I'd seen his Colt before. This time, I also noticed a badge affixed to his belt.

He's a rail marshal. What have I gotten myself into?

The Giant suddenly grabbed me, picked me up, and held me out in front of him. It startled me so much that I cried out. He had pockmarks on his face, his eyes were dark—almost black—and his breath smelled atrocious. I tried to push my body away from him, but that only made him hold on tighter. "Ya liddle shit. Ya don't mind well, do ya?" he barked.

"No, sir," I grunted.

He squeezed my sides tighter with his hands, making it hard for me to breathe. "Ya know what I do to ignorant liddle simps who don't do what I tell dem to?"

"Ouch!" I yelled, but it only made him squeeze tighter. His foul breath made me gag.

"I trow dem off da train!" he shouted then started to laugh. But it wasn't a funny laugh; it was maniacal—a crazy man's laugh.

My heart raced, and it wouldn't stop. Mom said I had a temper, and the Giant had made me angry. I was mad that I couldn't stop him from squeezing me. I was mad that I couldn't escape. And I was mad that I got caught. I hated the Giant. I wanted to hurt him. I wanted to bite him and kick him. Then, all of a sudden, I started yelling, and I couldn't stop myself.

"Yeah, well, you're a fartface!" I shouted at the top of my lungs. I had no conscience control over my mouth after that. "Pop says you're the company fartface! In fact, if anyone needs a good face fartin', yours is the face they fart on!" And then I added for good measure, "Fartface!" As soon as the words left my mouth, I was sorry I'd said what I said.

The Giant just stared at me blankly. Pop hadn't really called him the company fartface, I'd made that up on the spot. And in hindsight, it wasn't a very nice thing for me to do to throw Pop under the train like that. Pop probably didn't even know the guy. Even so, the Giant seemed confused, and for the first time, I thought I might be able to escape. So I raised my arms up then brought them down as hard as I could on the Giant's hands.

"Ha!" I yelled.

That accomplished nothing . . . except snapping the Giant out of his trance. He still held on to me just as tight. I hadn't escaped, and I was out of ideas.

After my attempted escape, something in the Giant's eyes changed, but he still had the look of a madman, and he smiled wider so I could see his yellow teeth. Then he trudged slowly over to the window and began to push me through it. I kicked at him and started yelling at him to stop, but I was only able to kick him a couple of times before he got ahold of both my legs. Then he started to push me out the window farther. I realized that he really was trying to throw me off the train—he was trying to kill me!

I screamed at the top of my lungs, flattened my back, and used my butt to jam myself in the window as best I could. But I was still hanging out the window, and the edges of the frame hurt as they cut into my skin. Then the Giant pulled me back in and laughed in my face. I still couldn't move my arms! With his hands on my shoulders, he jerked my head back and forth, in and out the window, shaking me like a rag doll and still laughing his crazy man's cackle. When a bug flew into my mouth, I started to cough.

The Giant continued to shake me and, at one point, my watch jiggled out of the pocket inside my jacket. It hung in the air right in front of me, but there was nothing I could do about it. Time slowed down as I watched it tumble end over end before bouncing off a railroad tie. It ricocheted into the rocks lining the tracks, hopped one more time, and then exploded into a million pieces. Pop had given the pocket watch to me for Christmas, and it was my favorite thing in the world. I shouted at the Giant again with renewed vigor, but I knew I couldn't keep fighting him for long. He was simply too strong.

When the train whistle shrieked again three times, I glanced ahead just in time to see the words *BIG TUNNEL* etched in stone. I kicked my legs even harder and screamed as loud as I could, "The tunnel! The tunnel!"

"Russ! Get down from there!" I heard Pop yell from inside the vestibule.

I looked up to see Pop coming through the door from the passenger car. The Giant turned slowly toward Pop and pulled me back inside the vestibule. Pop didn't appear angry, but he did look serious. I slid out of the window, ran over to him, and hugged him as hard as I could.

Then everything went dark as the train entered the tunnel. In the darkness, I heard the Giant's deep voice say, "I found him tryin' to climb out da window to da side of da car. He could've killed himself! What is he, a simp?"

I seethed with hatred for the Giant. I figured I was definitely in trouble and was worried that I'd gotten Pop into trouble too. Pop didn't say anything, though. He turned me around so my back was to him and put his hands on my shoulders. My entire body was quivering, but Pop was calm. Then he nudged me forward. He reached in front of me and opened the door to the passenger car. The lights were on in there, so I could see as Pop guided me slowly down the aisle and into one of the seats, where he sat down next to me. I still couldn't stop shaking.

Pop and I just stared at each other for a moment. He still didn't seem mad, but he just kept looking at me. "Sorry Pop," I finally said, breaking the silence. And I meant it. But I didn't know how to tell him about losing the pocket watch he'd given me for Christmas, so I didn't.

After what seemed like forever, Pop said, "Don't climb out of the train again, Russ. You could get hurt." His voice was soft. He didn't yell at me, and he didn't skin me. I scooted over and gave him a big hug. I felt safe with Pop.

"I thought he was going to kill me," I whispered.

Pop didn't say anything for a while. Then he responded, "He wasn't going to kill you, Russ. He was just trying to scare you."

Pop hadn't arrived 'til the end, so he didn't see and hear everything the Giant had said, but I kept quiet. I was just glad to be away from the Giant. I clung to Pop tightly until after the train exited the tunnel.

After a while, Pop cleared his throat and looked at me seriously. "Russ, today you're going to meet some new people in Mitchell. They're family," he explained.

It seemed like an odd statement for Pop to make. I'd met a lot of family members in Mitchell—aunts, uncles, and cousins—so many I couldn't keep track of them all. Mom said we were related to just about everyone in Two Counties. "Do I still get to see Birdy?" I asked.

Pop laughed and then he made our special sound, *Pop!*

I did it back. My *pop* wasn't as loud as his, but it was pretty darn powerful. "Yes, you will see a lot of Birdy," he assured me with a chuckle.

After a few moments, Pop became serious again, "You're also going to meet a new boy named Ray. He's older than you." I wanted to ask how much older, but Pop wasn't finished talking. "You see, Russ, you and Ray are brothers; you just haven't met yet. But you'll meet him at Uncle Walt's house."

"Yes, sir," I nodded. But I was very confused—it didn't make any sense. I knew boys back home with older brothers. But they all lived together and most of them shared a bedroom. Birdy had a younger brother named Frankie and they lived together. I liked the idea of having an older brother, though. It would be fun to have someone to play with at home when Pop wasn't around.

"Will he come live with us?" I asked.

"No. No. He lives with your grandma in Minnesota. He helps her out." Pop paused. I was having trouble wrapping my head around all this. "You'll also meet her later this evening. She's my mother . . . and Uncle Walt's too."

This was a lot for me to take in, but it was starting to make sense. "I would like to meet her," I said with a smile. Pop and I sat silently for a while. I had a million questions for him about my big brother and my grandma. I wondered what Ray looked like, and I wondered if he'd like me. Some of the older boys back home didn't like me. They often teased me and chased me home from school.

I also wondered what my grandma looked like. *Does Birdy know about my brother and my grandma? If my grandma is Uncle Walt's mom, that would make her Birdy's grandma, too, right?* But mostly, I wondered why Mom and Pop had never told me any of this before now. "Does my grandma know about me?" I asked.

Pop didn't answer; he just stared straight ahead. His mouth started moving like he was about to say something, but no sounds came out. I'd seen him do this before when he was thinking hard about something. Mom teased him about it, and he claimed he didn't do it, but he did. I wanted to ask him the question again, but I stopped. I was tired of talking.

I laid my head down on the armrest and closed my eyes. I felt tired and light-headed. I'd almost gotten myself killed. It had been the worst day of my life so far. But Pop rubbed my back like he did back home when I couldn't fall asleep. "I love you, boy," he whispered.

Pop, 1908

CHAPTER 4

Uncle Walt met us at the depot. The sun was out and the temperature was rising, even though it was still quite early in the morning. Pop and Uncle Walt shook hands, then Pop called him a dumb hayseed. Pop laughed when Uncle Walt told a naughty joke about a senator, a sailor, and a stripper, but I didn't get it. Pop told me I would understand someday. That only made Uncle Walt laugh harder.

Uncle Walt was older than Pop, but not by much. He was also a lot bigger. When he picked me up and gave me a big hug, my sides still hurt from the grip the Giant had had on me, but I didn't say anything. Pop was always in a good mood around Uncle Walt, and I didn't want to spoil it. As we walked through the depot, I tried to keep a low profile. I kept an eye out for the Giant. And I also kept my eyes peeled for Army and his four sisters, figuring they might be planning to beat me up for swiping his apple.

We rode to Birdy's new house in Uncle Walt's Model T. They used to live out in the country, near a bunch of woods and the East Fork of the White River. Back then, Birdy and I would sleep in a tent behind the house. But now they lived in town. Pop had shown me on the map. I was hoping that Birdy and I could explore Mitchell together.

Uncle Walt drove fast—even faster than Pop did back home! I knew all the names of the stores and shops in town, but it was hard to catch a glimpse of them while we were going what seemed to be a hundred miles an hour down the road. I did see Thompson's Drugstore, though. I saw a sign that said, "7 for 75¢," but I couldn't catch what was on sale. It didn't matter, though. I knew I could get an orange sodee pop there with Birdy, I just had to remember to ask Pop for some change.

At one point during the ride, I thought we were going to crash into a wagon. The farmer yelled at Uncle Walt, so he slammed on the car's horn. *AOOGA!* it blared. The farmer made a rude gesture, and Pop just laughed at it all. I was terrified the whole time. Thankfully, the drive was pretty short.

Birdy was standing in the front yard when we pulled in. He was hopping up and down, laughing, and pointing at me. He looked like he'd grown three feet since I saw him last, which wasn't that long ago. Birdy was always smiling. I jumped out of the car, ran over to him, and said hello. He gave me a firm handshake then put me in a headlock. That was Birdy's standard vaudevillian routine whenever we got together. Then he rubbed his knuckles on my head while I was still in a headlock. It didn't really hurt, though, because he didn't do it hard like the older boys back home. Birdy wasn't the smartest kid around, but he was the most happy-go-lucky. Even the older boys liked him.

On this particular day, there was a crowd at the house, and it seemed like everyone wanted to talk to Pop. I tried to find my brother, Ray, but I didn't know what he looked like. Plus, Birdy seemed excited to see me and wanted my attention. He was a bouncing Birdy.

Birdy tried to talk but was out of breath from bouncing and wrestling with me. "Dad said we can hang out with the older boys today. Isn't that swell?" Birdy wheezed. "So don't be all sad and shit, Russ. Ya hear me knucklehead?" Birdy slugged me and burst out laughing. He had the funniest laugh in Two Counties.

Just then, I heard the porch door slam behind me. "Russ, get yourself over here!" Aunt Vinney yelled. She was Birdy's mom, and I had a crush on her something fierce. She had red hair as bright as the sun, and she was my favorite aunt in the whole world. I planned on marrying her someday.

I ran up the steps of the front porch and gave her a big hug. When she gave me about a million kisses, I didn't even wipe them off. She was a country girl, for sure. She said things like "warshed" instead of "washed" and "that'll be a fine how dee do."

"Are ya hungry?" she asked.

"Yes ma'am," I answered.

"There's flapjacks and bacon in the kitchen. We done ate, so eat all ya want," she replied nodding toward the front door.

"I figured Birdy had already eaten everything," I teased her and Birdy at the same time.

She giggled and said, "Go inside to Birdy's room and take off your fancy traveling clothes. I laid out some runnin' around clothes for ya."

"I see you're wearing your fancy town dress. You look radiant this morning," I said, laying it on thick.

"Oh my! You're quite the ladies' man. I'm gonna keep you here from now on. There's a pair of Birdy's old overalls on the bed and a pair of boots on the back porch. Take off your jacket and just wear your shirt 'round."

She looked over at Birdy and then glanced back at me with that smile and those crazy green eyes. Then she leaned down and whispered in my ear, "If y'all end up shootin' guns today and ya get the opportunity, go ahead and shoot Birdy for me, will ya? We just can't afford to feed him no more."

She must've seen the shocked look on my face because she gave me a wink and a peck on the cheek, then she did a pirouette off the front porch and landed in the middle of a gaggle of gals who were also dressed in their finest town attire. They all shared hugs and kisses. I stared at Aunt Vinney's tight-fitting dress for a little too long before I turned back to Birdy. He was still laughing at what she'd said about shooting him. Then he slapped me on the back of the head and ran into the house.

I hadn't been to this house before, but the furniture was the same. It was a two-story like our house back home. Birdy ran up the stairs near the front door, but I didn't follow him. I smelled food, so I made a detour and followed my nose into the kitchen.

Aunt Vinney's kitchen wasn't as big as ours back home, but it was bigger than the one she'd had out in the country. On the counter sat a plate with some bacon and one with flapjacks. I waved away the swarm of flies who were also having breakfast, then I picked up two flapjacks and three pieces of bacon and started shoving food into my mouth with both hands. It tasted so good, I just couldn't help myself. Aunt Vinney could cook a mean breakfast, which was just one of the many things I loved about her.

"Russ!" Birdy yelled from upstairs. "Stop moseyin'!"

I turned and ran for the stairs, still gobbling up the food I'd taken as I climbed the steps two at a time. I found Birdy in his room, staring out the front window.

"I wonder what's goin' on. Just about everybody in Two Counties is here," he commented. "The only thing missing is a band and we could be havin' us a hootenanny."

I shrugged my shoulders. I didn't care about stuff like that. I finished my flapjack and crammed another piece of bacon into my mouth. Then I stripped down to my underwear and put on Birdy's old overalls. They were too big for me, but I adjusted the straps until they stayed up. It felt good to get out of my city clothes. When I saw two beds, I realized that Birdy had to share a room with his little brother, Frankie.

"Do you remember our cousins?" Birdy asked. I needed a few more details before I could say for sure.

When I shook my head, he continued, "Well, you'll meet 'em in a bit. They got out of doin' fieldwork today 'cause Ray's in town. If Ray wasn't here, they'd ditch us for sure."

I walked over to the window and looked out. "Which one's Ray?" I asked.

"What do you mean?" Birdy asked. "He's right there." I followed Birdy's outstretched finger with my eyes to a group of three teenage boys. I studied each of them. I recognized the boy on the end immediately. He'd picked on me the last time I'd seen him, which was at least a year earlier. For a moment, I thought he was Ray, but then I remembered his name was Nathan. I also recognized the boy on the left, the smallest of the three. He was Nathan's younger brother, Josie. But the tall boy in the middle was different. He looked like a taller, younger version of Pop. I couldn't take my eyes off him.

Birdy grabbed the last piece of bacon out of my hand. "Can't you see him, Russ? Maybe you need glasses," Birdy teased. "I know a kid at school who got glasses. Some of the kids pick on him and call him four eyes, but I stick up for him."

"I never met him before," I said. Ray was a tall, good-looking teenager with an easygoing smile. He wore his dark hair slicked back just like Pop. As I watched the group of boys, I noticed the other two trying to get Ray's attention. They smiled when Ray talked to them. *I sure hope he likes me*, I thought.

Birdy laughed. "Wait, are you tryin' to tell me you don't know your own brother, Russ? That's a good one."

"No, I don't," I replied with a hint of sadness in my voice.

When I turned back to Birdy, his face became more serious. "Wow, Russ! If you're jokin', I'm gonna punch you real hard!"

"I'm not, Birdy. I swear. Pop just told me about him on the train ride here." I kept watching Ray as he interacted with Nathan and Josie. *I wonder what he's like*, I thought. Seeing him made me think about the older boys back home who picked on me.

"You're full of it, Russ! I've told you stuff about Ray before. I must've."

I turned around and looked at Birdy again. I was about to say that he hadn't, but then I thought about it. Birdy talked about everybody, so I figured it was possible that he'd mentioned Ray. But most of the time, I had no idea who he was talking about when he told stories. Besides, a lot of people around here had the same last names. Pop said all of Two Counties was rotten with our kin . . . and Kentucky too.

"Maybe you did mention him," I said. "But I'm sure you never once told me he was my brother."

"Wow! That's a doozy, Russ! I had no idea you didn't know. I'm sorry."

"It's OK, Birdy. I'm not mad."

Birdy and I continued to look out the window. "Ray lives in Minnesota, and he lived in Texas before that. When he was younger, he lived a short walk from here. But Ray visits a lot, especially in the summer. All the older boys . . . *and* girls . . . like him."

"Ew," I grimaced.

"You're funny, Russ," Birdy chuckled as he put me in a headlock again. But he let me go quick, so I didn't punch him.

I saw Pop walk over to Ray and the other boys. I couldn't hear what they were saying, but Pop shook hands with all of them, then the other boys walked away. Ray nodded his head a couple of times as Pop talked. Ray was taller than Pop! Pop handed Ray something, but I couldn't tell what it was. Then Pop gave him a hug, and Ray smiled slightly. They talked for a little while longer before going their separate ways.

Birdy and I looked at each other, trying to decipher what we'd just witnessed. Birdy just shrugged his shoulders then turned and ran out of his room and down the stairs. I looked out the window for a few more minutes. It was strange to see Pop with another son. It made me feel sad, and I again wondered why I had never met Ray before. It was a lot to think about, and it didn't make any sense, so I turned and left Birdy's room munching on the last flapjack.

I made my way to the back porch and put on Birdy's old boots. They were a little bit big, but they were broken in and comfortable. I looked like a country boy dressed to go work in the fields. I yelled "Howdy!" in my best country boy voice as I jumped down off the porch. It was only then that I noticed Birdy, Ray, and the other boys standing under a tree in the backyard. And they were all staring at me like I was the bearded lady at the circus. I froze, wide-eyed.

Luckily, Aunt Vinney saved me when she called for Birdy from the front yard, but he just kept staring at me like the other guys. "Birdy!" she yelled again, this time loud enough for everyone in Two Counties to hear her. Birdy glanced over his shoulder, said something to the older boys, and then turned and ran toward the front yard. I watched him run around the side of the house.

When I looked over at the older boys, they were still staring at me. I figured I'd better go introduce myself and try to make a better second impression. And, since I was a young man, it was the polite thing to do. As I walked toward them, I made eye contact with Ray. He wasn't smiling, but he didn't look mad, either.

"Damn, Ray. . . . He looks just like you!" Nathan remarked. Then he said to me, "Hey, Runt, come here. I remember you." When I walked over to them, he said, "Howdy! You remember me? I'm Nathan."

I shook his hand. He didn't look me in the eye, but his handshake was firm. "I'm Russ," I said.

"I know what your name is, Runt," Nathan continued. Then, gesturing toward Josie, he said, "This low-down, no-good scoundrel here is my little brother, Josie." I chuckled and shook Josie's hand.

"Hey, Runt, I remember you too," Josie said. I guessed that was going to be my nickname. "My brother Nathan's kind of feebleminded, so you might have to tell him things three or four times," Josie snickered. I didn't understand the joke, but it sounded funny, so I laughed too.

Nathan punched Josie in the arm, and both immediately assumed a boxer's stance. While they were fixing to go at it, I turned to Ray. He examined me with a curious look on his face. I decided the best thing to do was to be polite. I figured there was no sense getting off on the wrong foot with him. "Hi, Ray. . . . Uh, I guess I'm your brother, Russ. I'm glad to finally meet you."

Nathan and Josie repeated what I said and laughed, trying to make me angry. That's what the older boys did back home too—and it was working. Pop told me it was best to just ignore them when they did that, but it was easier said than done.

When Ray scowled at Nathan and Josie, they stopped laughing. Then he looked at me and smiled. His voice was deep but not loud. "Nice to meet ya, kid." He shook my hand firmly and looked me in the eyes. I was happy that Ray liked me.

Birdy fell as he came bounding around the corner of the house. He got back up and almost fell again before staggering over to us. I laughed at him along with the other boys. "Birdy's gonna be a professional dancer, ya know," Nathan quipped.

"Graceful as a gazelle," Josie joked.

"OK, OK," Birdy gasped. We waited while he tried to catch his breath. "OK, I didn't want you guys to leave without me. So where are we going?"

"Rebel Joe's cave," Ray answered. Nathan and Josie smirked and nodded. Rebel Joe's cave sounded like a scary place to me. I didn't know who Rebel Joe was, but I hoped he wasn't home.

Nathan grabbed Birdy by the shirt and hissed, "And if you throw up again, Birdy, I'll give you a bloody nose."

"Come on," Birdy retorted, "I had the stomach sickness that time. I'll be fine."

Ray put on his gambler hat and started walking away. Both Nathan and Josie put on their matching straw hats. Nathan looked at me and then said to Birdy, "He'll keep his mouth shut, won't he?"

"Yeah, Russ never ratted out anyone," Birdy replied. Then he gave me a wide-eyed look.

"Yeah, I'm not a rat," I said. I didn't know what they were talking about, but I promised not to tell anyone about it. Nathan didn't seem convinced, but he shrugged then ran ahead to catch up with Ray and Josie.

I laughed when Birdy made a funny face at me. He handed me a newsboy cap identical to his own, except that it was brown instead of gray. I put it on then followed him as he ran after the older boys. When we caught up with them, we gave them some space. They seemed to be catching Ray up on events since he'd last visited. It was all so strange to be walking behind my brother—a brother whom I'd just met. Two Counties seemed different on this day, different from any other day I'd visited. Everything felt mixed up and confusing.

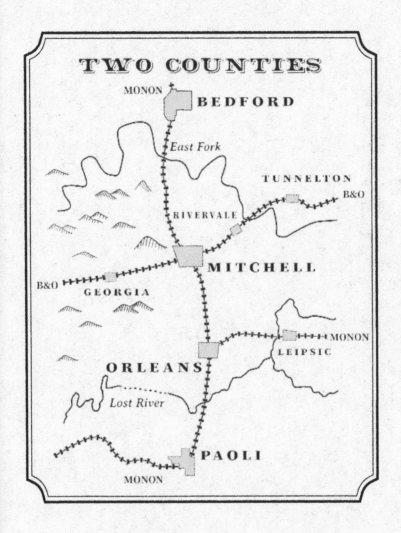

CHAPTER 5
Friday, June 13, 1924, 8:26 a.m.
Two Counties

Birdy and his family lived on the outskirts of town, so after crossing a few streets, a set of railroad tracks, and a large crick, we were out in the country. We followed the train tracks west out of town. There was a large patch of woods on one side and a cornfield on the other. It was hard for me to tell if something was a big hill with trees or just a large grove of tall trees. The corn was just starting to sprout out of the ground in the fields we passed, and the trees were finally in full bloom. I was glad to be done with school for the summer.

Birdy reminded me again that I couldn't tell Pop what we were going to do. He said if I did, the older boys wouldn't let us hang around them anymore and that they'd probably beat me up. That didn't sound very fun. I had kept secrets from Mom and Pop before, so I said, "That's easy."

Birdy smiled and patted me on the back before joining the older boys. I hung back for a minute and reached for my pocket watch to see what time it was. But then I remembered that it had fallen off the train. I figured I'd have to eventually tell Pop that I lost it, but I never wanted to talk about the Giant again. After shuddering at the thought of him, I ran to catch up to Birdy and the older boys.

"They won the state championship three years in a row! No one had ever done that before—it's practically impossible!" Nathan exclaimed, arguing with Josie. "So yes, I'm saying that no one will ever win three state championships in a row ever again, you dumbass. I'll betcha a dollar."

"You don't have a dollar!" Ray chuckled.

"Well, if I did . . . ," Nathan said.

I knew Nathan and Josie were talking about basketball, even though I was probably the only kid in Indiana who didn't know a lick about the game—probably Kentucky too. Like many of the boys at home, Birdy could rattle off names, towns, and mascots as he talked about the games. He knew the scores and the big shots. I knew where most of the towns were from my maps, but not much else.

The older boys had been talking about basketball on and off since we'd left the house. I wanted to join in and silently wished I knew more about the game, but I'd never even played it. I wanted to ask the older boys questions about it but decided not to. I didn't want them to think I was stupid—or a sissy. Maybe if I read the sports pages in the newspaper once I got back home—like Pop did—I could talk to them better next time.

Suddenly, we heard a loud gunshot far off in the distance. "Model 8," Ray announced. Josie and Nathan agreed. Birdy told me once that country boys played a game to see who could guess the type of rifle from the sound of the gunshot it made. Whoever said it first, won. Clearly, Ray had played this game before.

Somebody was hunting out there, but it was far away, so we kept walking. I was getting a bit tired, but then Nathan mentioned something I was familiar with, so I started paying attention. "Milton's dad bought a Model T too," he said.

"Yeah, but he wrecked it two days later," Josie howled. "He was showing off, seeing how fast he could go, and he hit a tree stump."

Ray shook his head and laughed.

"Birdy, I heard Milton's dad asked Uncle Walt to fix it," Nathan said.

"Yep," Birdy replied proudly. "Dad let me help him too. He's been teaching me how to fix cars."

"Pop's been teaching me how to work on his Model T too!" I chimed in, excited that I could talk about cars with the other boys.

Birdy continued, "Dad fixed it up yesterday after we got the parts delivered. After Milton's old man picked it up, Dad told me he would likely wreck it again in two days . . . three tops."

"Did ya get to turn the crank?" asked Josie, impressed.

"No. Dad said it would yank my arm off," Birdy replied dejectedly.

I glanced over at Ray. He was looking at me but also kind of looking off into space. He reminded me so much of Pop. He looked away when he noticed I was watching him.

"

I drive Grandpa Marker's Studebaker up in Minnesota now," Ray bragged.

"No way!" Nathan and Josie exclaimed at the same time.

"Yep," Ray said.

They asked him how fast he went and for how long. I'd never heard of Grandpa Marker before. I figured he might be married to my grandma. Pop had said that Ray lived with her, but he hadn't mentioned a grandpa. I wanted to ask Ray about this Grandpa Marker, but the older boys started talking about basketball again, and I missed my chance.

"My older cousin Jimbo—well, I guess he's *our* cousin, you remember him—anyway, he knows most of the guys on the Bloomington team that won the state championship years back," Nathan boasted. "He said they all got drunk on the Rebel Joe the night after the game, but the coach found out and made them practice the next day. Can you believe that? The coach made them practice *after* they'd already won the state championship! Jimmy told me a couple of the guys threw up, and the coach made the entire team clean it up. They were all gagging and yacking!"

There were groans all around. "I heard that, too, but I don't believe it," Josie admitted. "What kind of coach would make the players practice *after* they'd won?"

"No, I heard about it too," Ray said, "and it really happened." That seemed to end the debate. If Ray said it happened, then it happened.

"Geez, that's one tough coach," Birdy groaned. "I hope I never have a coach like that."

At that point, we'd made our way to a pasture of tallgrass and wildflowers. The field was full of hundreds of flowers of various colors and species, but it was suddenly strange not to see corn. The grass came up to my knees. I had no idea where we were going but was happy to hang out with Birdy and the older boys.

As we made our way through the pasture, Birdy warned me to be careful not to step in any cow pies. He tried to point them out as we trudged along. A little while later, he said to me, "We ain't too far from Rebel Joe's cave."

"Who's Rebel Joe?" I inquired.

As the older boys laughed at me, Nathan put his hands on my shoulders from behind and said, "Only the best whiskey in Two Counties, kid."

"Hooch?" I asked. "Are you guys going to drink some hooch?"

"How old are ya, Runt?" Nathan asked.

"Ten," I yelled out.

"No, you're not," Ray said softly without turning around.

A cold chill went down my spine. Ray had caught me in my big lie. I'd been telling everyone for the last week I was ten. But that wasn't entirely true. I wouldn't turn ten until late fall. *How did Ray know?* I glanced over at Nathan, who was scowling at me, and then at Josie, who had a puzzled look on his face. I hoped I didn't get muddled right then and there. And I wondered if the older boys might slap me around for lying to them. Or worse, ditch me like the mean kids back home.

Nathan grabbed my shirt, "You lying to me, boy?"

"I . . . uh . . . ," was all I could get out.

I tried to break free, but Nathan had ahold of me good. I looked up at Birdy who was looking back at me with a concerned look on his face, but then he smiled and winked at me.

"Ray!" Birdy whined, as he ran and caught up with Ray who'd continued walking. "If Russ gets to be ten, then I get to be eleven 'cause I turn eleven before Russ turns ten. That's only fair!"

Ray looked at Birdy for a moment with an exasperated look on his face. Then he pushed Birdy down with one hand, "I really don't give a damn."

"Yes!" Birdy shouted, as he jumped up and bounded backward to the rest of us. He took three long hops, made three loud whoops, and then circled back behind Nathan. He looked like a cartoon character from the picture show.

Then out of nowhere, Birdy jumped on Nathan's back and hollered, "Wrestling match!" Nathan let go of me, causing me to fall and land on my butt. Nathan spun around trying to dislodge Birdy, who had his arms and legs wrapped around him good.

"*Ding!*" yelled Josie.

"I'm eleven now, Nathan! Woo-hoo! Ride 'em cowboy! Yeehaw!"

Nathan cussed a bunch and spun around and around, but he couldn't get Birdy off his back. After a while, Nathan tripped and fell with Birdy still on his back. I thought for a moment that Birdy might've actually had a chance to win.

"Pin him, Birdy!" Josie shouted. It surprised me for a moment that Josie would root against his own brother, but then I remembered that it was Nathan.

As Nathan rocked from side to side, he eventually escaped Birdy's grasp. He was bigger than Birdy, but not by much. After about a minute, Nathan managed to get on top of Birdy and pin him. Josie counted to three, and just like that, the match was over. "I'm still the champion!" Nathan yelled to no one in particular.

Ray impatiently cleared his throat in front of us.

"Well, of my weight class anyway," Nathan clarified.

Josie helped Birdy up and comforted him a bit, "You almost had him."

"No, he didn't," Nathan said as he shoved Josie out of the way.

"You should've used the arm bar on him when you had the chance!" Josie said.

"I can't use the arm bar on my own cousin," Birdy replied.

"I would've," Josie said.

"I'm going to use the arm bar on you when we get home," Nathan shouted back.

Birdy winked at me again. It was then that I realized he'd jumped on Nathan to divert his attention from me. And it seemed to have worked because in all the excitement, Nathan forgot about me. Josie walked over and helped me up. Nathan ran ahead to catch up with Ray, while Birdy, Josie, and I brought up the rear.

"You know what this means, Russ?" Birdy asked.

"No," I replied.

"Since Ray said it was OK for me to be eleven, it means you can be ten!"

"And you know what that means?" Josie asked.

I shook my head.

"It means you're old enough to have a sip of the Rebel Joe," Birdy responded.

"Yeah, it's like an initiation or something," Josie said. "I had my first sip before I turned ten too."

"I love me a good sip of the Rebel Joe," Birdy shouted.

Ray turned around and glared at Birdy. "Yeah, but you also threw up all over the place the last time you had a sip. And you almost got us all a good skinnin'! Uncle Walt can slap a mean belt when he wants too."

"I told you, it wasn't the Rebel Joe that made me sick!" Birdy countered. "You'll be alright, won't you, Russ?"

"Oh sure. I've drunk out of Pop's glass lots of times," I lied—I hadn't had a drop of alcohol my entire life. Ray shot me a look that let me know he wasn't buying it. But he didn't say anything, he just shrugged.

Birdy elbowed me in the ribs and scolded, "Just don't tell Pop, OK? Ray's right. We'll all get a good whippin' if the grown-ups find out."

"I keep secrets better than anyone," I said.

Nathan and Josie laughed and nodded to each other. "You're a good guy, Runt," Nathan said as he smacked me on the back of the head.

I wanted to tell them all that Pop would never skin anybody. He'd never skinned me before, even when I got into big trouble—like when I crawled out of the train earlier that morning.

51

I wondered what liquor would taste like. Even though I'd never tasted alcohol before, I *had* smelled it, and it smelled awful. But I didn't want the guys to think I was a little boy if I didn't drink it. I was ten in Two Counties, so I had to act the part. *I wonder why they called it Rebel Joe?* I thought. *Mom calls Pop's drink whiskey. Ray said we're going to Rebel Joe's cave. Maybe that's where they go to secretly drink whiskey? It was a lot to think about.*

We followed a path that headed south, away from the railroad tracks. As we continued to walk, I realized that I'd lost my sense of direction. Even though I didn't recognize anything familiar, I thought I kind of knew what direction town was. I figured it was still behind us, but I wasn't sure at this point. Every now and again, I'd hear the scream from a train whistle in the distance. Sometimes it sounded close, sometimes it seemed far away. I hoped I wouldn't get separated from the guys and get lost.

I sprinted ahead and caught up to Ray at the front of the pack then tried to think of something to say. "Do you have a rifle back home?" I asked.

"Yeah, I got a .22," he replied with a smile.

"Pop says I can't have a rifle because we live in town." Ray nodded but didn't say anything. "Do you and Pop go fishing?" I asked, trying to keep the conversation going.

"No," Ray answered swiftly with a hint of anger in his voice. He just kept looking straight ahead.

"Pop and I go fishing sometimes," I continued. "We go to the East Fork. I've caught bluegill, bass, and even a flathead once!"

"It's called the White River," Ray corrected.

"Pop won't call it the White River," I added. "He says the East Fork is the most perfect river in the world—the best one ever—and the West Fork is nothing but a wide crick that's connected to a bunch of sewers. In fact, he says they really aren't the same river at all and some Frenchman back in the olden days drew his map wrong. Pop even said that if you cast your line in the West Fork, you're bound to hook a turd rather than a fish."

"Ew," Birdy said. Nathan and Josie laughed at Birdy.

"Yeah? Well, good for you and Pop," Ray sneered as he sped up and walked away from me.

I wasn't sure what that was all about, but I figured I had at least talked to him for a bit one-on-one. *I guess I'll try again later*. Birdy walked up beside me, stretched out his hands in front of me and said, "I caught a turd this big once."

We all laughed at him, except for Ray.

When we came to a narrow path in the pasture, we had to walk single file. It took me a minute, but then I realized we were walking in age order. Ray went first—as I was sure he was the oldest—then Nathan, Josie, Birdy, and me. I knew how old Birdy was, but I didn't know how old the other boys were. But I figured I had it right.

I was just about to ask when I heard and felt something fly past my head making a loud whizzing sound. Then the ground in front of me exploded with dirt going everywhere. A moment later, I heard a loud gunshot really close to us. The other boys dropped to their bellies, but I froze. Soon, two more whizzing sounds went by and two more shots ricocheted off the ground right in front of me, then two more gunshots rang out.

"Get the hell down!" Ray barked. I fell to the ground like the other boys had, but I wished I'd picked a better spot. There was a cow pie right in front of my face. It smelled horrible, and flies were swarming all over it. But at least I hadn't landed right on it.

"Stop shooting!" Ray shouted. "Stop shooting!"

I fixed my eyes on Ray. He didn't seem frightened, but he did look concerned. When I glanced over at Nathan and Josie, they were sticking their heads up a bit and looking around. I could tell they were both afraid. Birdy was lying flat on his stomach with his face in the dirt and his hands over his ears. He was *really* scared.

Ray hollered again, "Call out!" His voice boomed like a grown man's. After a moment, Ray stood up and looked around, but he motioned for all of us to stay down. That was fine with me. I realized I could've been shot. It was the second time in one day that I'd cheated death. As far as I was concerned, this time, Ray had saved my life.

I hoped the hunters had heard Ray and stopped shooting. We remained on the ground for what seemed like forever. I wanted to get away from the stinky cow pie that was making me gag, but I knew I should stay put until Ray told me otherwise.

"I'll kill you if I find you!" Ray finally yelled in the direction of the gunshots.

Ray was scary when he was mad.

"Dammit! They never acknowledged," Ray grumbled. Then he turned to us and said, "I don't see or hear 'em, so I guess they've moved on." He looked around one more time then motioned for us to get up. "Let's get to the cave before they start shooting again."

"It was probably a bunch of drunk morons," Nathan groused.

Once we were all on our feet, Ray led us toward a large tree line up ahead. "What kind of rifle was that?" I asked Birdy.

Birdy shrugged his shoulders. So did Nathan and Josie. "I was too scared to think about it," Josie confessed.

"Me too. But at least I didn't shit myself like Runt here," Nathan taunted.

"I didn't shit myself! I almost fell on a cow pie." I explained as I pointed to the back of my overalls. "See, no shit stains." Everyone laughed at that—everyone except for Ray.

Ray continued to stare straight ahead. "It was a Winchester Model 94," he responded flatly.

I walked alongside Birdy as we headed for the woods ahead of us. I wanted to take my mind off the hunters and my most recent near-death experience, so I tried to think of something to say. "Hey, Birdy, . . . Pop said I get to spend the night at your house tonight. We leave tomorrow on the daily 68, so I get to stay all day and all night."

"That's great! We can sleep in the backyard. We just need to put up the tent, but it won't take long. My dad will help us."

"That sounds like fun!" I replied.

When we finally made it into the woods, we walked in single file along a well-worn path. Sometimes there wasn't even a path, just an area where the undergrowth had been trampled down.

Nobody talked to each other for a while. I could hear birds singing from every tree, and it took my eyes some time to adjust to the darker surroundings. I was exhausted but didn't say anything. I hoped we would stop soon and take a break.

After a while, we came to a fast-flowing stream in a deep ravine. I looked down into it and named the ravine the Grand Chasm. On our side of the ravine, one enormous tree towered over the others. The tree was so tall, I couldn't even see the top. One of the tree's larger branches forked outward and reached across the ravine. A rope was tied to the branch and hung down about five feet above the stream. It made me wonder how anyone could've climbed up there to tie the rope—and I was a good tree climber.

All of a sudden, Ray was sprinting toward the ravine. When he came to the edge, he leaped into the air. As he plummeted, he reached out, grabbed ahold of the rope, and climbed up it arm over arm, kicking his feet out to swing back and forth. When he neared the sides of the Grand Chasm, he flattened his body to avoid crashing. As he gained momentum, he rocked back and forth—higher and higher like a pendulum—for what seemed like a few minutes as he straddled the rope. Then he swung past us, jumped toward the ground, and threw the rope to Nathan. Ray landed on his feet and struck the landing like a circus acrobat.

"Wow!" I raved with a look of awe on my face. "That was incredible, Ray!"

Ray gave me a huge, satisfied grin.

Nathan's swing wasn't quite as impressive as Ray's, but it sure looked like fun. After a few rides back and forth, he tossed the rope to Josie and sailed to the ground. When it was Birdy's turn, he kicked his legs up over his head and swung upside down!

"Wow!" I said, amazed.

"Show off!" Nathan jeered. Birdy stayed upside down for a few swings before flipping over to right himself. As he flew back over where we were standing, he let go of the rope and landed pretty far away from the Grand Chasm.

Ray grabbed the rope before it swayed back over the ravine. He threw it to me, but I missed it. I felt like a baby for that. Ray looked disappointed, but he quickly grabbed the rope and handed it to me. In a soft voice he said, "Just hold onto the rope with both hands and run as fast as you can. Whatever you do, don't let go of the rope. You hear me? *Don't* let go of the rope! When you get to the other side, just turn your body, and you'll swing right back."

I looked at Ray somberly and nodded. It felt nice to have him help me. I looked back at Birdy, and he gave me an encouraging smile. I held on as tight as I could, ran toward the ravine, kicked up my legs, and, suddenly, I was flying over the stream. I felt like Tarzan, so I let loose with his famous yell. It was much higher up than I'd imagined it would be, and I was going a lot faster than I expected to, and the water racing below me terrified me, but it was incredible!

Once I got to the other side of the Grand Chasm, I turned my body around just like Ray had told me to, then I kicked out my legs, and swung back toward the others. I was scared to let go of the rope and jump off, but I didn't want them to know that, so I released it and tried to jump as far as I could with my arms and legs flailing through the air. When I hit the ground, I tripped and tumbled head over feet.

Everyone laughed at me, and Nathan called me a rookie, but I didn't care. It was the most exhilarating thing I'd ever done in my entire life! Birdy came running over and helped me up. "I wanna do it again!" I cheered.

"You'll get your chance, Rookie," Nathan assured.

We took turns swinging across the Grand Chasm a few more times. On his fourth turn, Ray even copied Birdy and went upside down. But this time, he jumped off on the other side of the ravine.

Nathan tried to go upside down too, but without much success. Nathan, Josie, and Birdy all took their turns and landed on the other side of the Grand Chasm.

After Birdy took his final turn, Ray grabbed the rope and called over to me, "OK, Russ. Grab the rope when it comes over, then swing over to this side. You can do this, Russ."

I was bound and determined to grab the rope when it came my way, and this time, I did it. As I took off over the Grand Chasm, I tried to kick my feet over my head and go upside down, but I ended up just flipping over, so I gave up. When I was on the other side, I threw the rope while I was in the air. I landed on my feet, but I had so much momentum going that I rolled over backward. The others laughed at me again, except for Ray, who held out his hand to help me up. I grabbed his hand and popped up.

"I wanna do it again!" I said excitedly.

"Fine by me, kid. Stay and swing," Ray muttered. Then he turned around and began walking in the other direction. The rest of the guys followed. "Let's swing some more, Birdy!" I exclaimed.

Birdy looked up at the guys walking away and whispered, "Don't act like a little kid, Russ. They won't let us hang out with them if you start acting like a baby."

I didn't know what to do. Swinging on the rope was more fun than being with anyone—including Birdy and the older boys. I thought about staying there the whole day and just swinging by myself. I liked being alone sometimes. But I also wanted to stay with Ray and Birdy. I just wished we could've stayed and swung on the rope all day.

"Come on, Russ," Birdy said as he began to walk away. I took one last look at the rope swaying slowly back and forth and left the Grand Chasm behind.

Chapter 6

After trekking through the woods for a few more minutes, we came to a shallower ravine with a small brook running through it. We followed the brook a bit upstream, and I stopped when the rest of the guys came to a halt. I gasped when I saw the cave for the first time. The cave's entrance wasn't tall, but I figured it was high enough for me to walk inside. However, it was also covered with barbed wire fencing, and that—coupled with the brook meandering inside— gave the cave an eerie and evil feel.

"Welcome to Rebel Joe's cave," Birdy said to me, grinning from ear to ear with his arms wide open.

Rebel Joe's cave scared the shit out of me. "Why is it fenced off?" I asked.

Josie spoke up, "Uncle Isom don't want no one goin' in. It's his land, I think. He chased us away once last summer."

"Which Uncle Isom?" Birdy asked.

"The mean one. He told our dad and we got a good skinnin' for it," Nathan said.

"How do you get in?" I questioned.

Nathan chuckled, then Ray and Josie did too. They all glanced at Ray, who gave me a sly smile and motioned for me to follow him into the brook. He stepped down onto a flat rock sticking up out of the water. I could tell the brook wasn't very deep, and I figured that since I was wearing Birdy's boots, I could splash through it easily. But as I followed Ray, I soon realized that I didn't need to. Ray stepped on large flat stones all the way to the cave's entrance and didn't get his boots wet once.

Ray stopped outside the cave and pointed to some long pieces of wood forming a frame that held the barbed wire snuggly against the mouth of the cave. "You see, Uncle Isom did a good job drilling those bolts into the stone. Come to think of it, he probably didn't do it himself. He must have some stonecutters in the family because the bolts hold these four-by-fours to that rock face tight. You'd need dynamite to get that wood off," Ray explained.

"Can't you cut through the fence with wire cutters?" I inquired.

Ray slapped me on the back of the head.

"Ouch!" I yelped.

"I can't fix broken barbed wire, kid. Besides, next time Uncle Isom comes down here, he'll see we did it, and then that wouldn't do us any good, now would it?"

"And I'd probably get another skinnin', so I'd owe you a knuckle sandwich, Runt," Nathan added.

I realized Ray was right, but I had no idea what Nathan was babbling about.

Ray pointed up to corner where the boards came together, "He attached the barbed wire to a smaller fence post here and over there along both sides. He probably did the work back in his barn. To connect the boards bolted to the stone and the posts with the barbed wire, he only used two nails, one on the top and on the bottom to fix 'em together. Probably figured it was good enough. Rather shortsighted on his part, wouldn't ya say?"

I nodded, but I wasn't following.

"So, if someone were to use a big hammer claw to get the nails free here and here," Ray said, pointing at small holes in the wood where nails had once been, "then you'd just need to bend the board 'round this rock here where it fits snug, give it a good shove, and well, well . . . ," Ray nudged the barbed wire fencing free from the cave's entrance. Then he picked up the post with both hands and backed up as he kept the barbed wire taut. Finally, he walked slowly to the other side of the entrance and placed the post up against the stone face.

"Open sesame!" Birdy cheered.

"Well, whaddaya know . . . we got us a private speakeasy, y'all!" Josie exclaimed.

"Wow!" I muttered.

Ray gave me a smile, then he pointed to the entrance, "Go on in then."

"No way, Ray!" I shouted without thinking. The rest of the guys howled at me—even Birdy. I sounded like a scaredy-cat for sure.

"Get outta my way, Runt," Nathan ordered as he pushed past me and into the cave, ducking down as he entered. Ray followed him inside, shaking his head and chuckling at me as he walked by.

Josie went next, then Birdy patted me on the back and said, "C'mon . . . just walk on the rocks like I do."

I did, but it took my eyes a moment to adjust to the darkness of the cave. It was narrow toward the entrance but widened the farther we went inside. As we continued going deeper inside, I could see the fellas up ahead. They were drinking from a small waterfall cascading down from the roof of the cave. *Maybe that's the source of the brook.* I'd always wondered what the source of the East Fork looked like—I hoped it looked like this. As I got closer to the bubbling waterfall, the cave widened even more, and it was easier to make my way.

When I caught up to the others, I stood behind Birdy, who was drinking handfuls of the crisp, cool water. There wasn't enough room for everyone, so I waited politely to take my turn, but I was thirsty too.

When Birdy finished getting his fill, he turned back to me and said, "It's clean, so you can drink from it. There's no pig farms upstream."

I cupped my hands to catch the water and drank vigorously. The water made a pleasant noise as it splashed into the brook. It masked the conversation the fellas were having behind me. For a moment, I forgot all about them as I listened to the soft sound of the waterfall. After a while, Birdy tapped on my back and brought me back to reality. He pointed his thumb in the direction of the guys, who were making their way deeper into the cave.

As I walked farther back into the cave, I noticed that the brook was getting deeper. At this point, it was about a foot deep, but I could still walk alongside it and keep my boots dry. I followed Birdy until we came to what appeared to be the back of the cave. But then Ray started climbing up the back of the cave and disappeared. Nathan did the same. I looked back and noticed that we were about fifteen to twenty feet from the cave's entrance. And because my eyes were still adjusting to the light, the cave looked even creepier than when we'd first arrived.

"It's easy to climb, Russ," Birdy encouraged. "Just grab ahold of the rocks as you climb. It's not high."

I looked up and noticed Josie shimmying up a smaller shaft that went inside the top of the cave. Then he quickly disappeared into another passageway. Birdy went next, and then I followed, trying to mimic Birdy's movements. As promised, it was an easy climb, and when I made it to the top, Birdy held out his hand and pulled me into what I presumed to be the next tunnel. It was pitch-black, so I stood still.

Ray lit a match and asked, "Who has the candle?"

"Here ya go," Josie said as he handed Ray a small candle. "I had to swipe it from the house. We can leave it here, though, . . . for next time."

Ray nodded and lit the candle. Josie cupped his hands around the flame until it was steady, then Ray put out the match with a wave of his hand and sat down on a large rock. Nathan took a seat next to him. Josie sat across from his brother, and before I could do anything, Birdy sat down across from Ray, which was where I wanted to sit. I thought about asking Birdy if he'd switch with me, but when Ray glanced at me, I decided not to cause a fuss.

I could see the cavern better with the candle burning and the light coming from the shaft we'd shimmied up. It looked to me like a bunch of large rocks had fallen over in the back of the cave, which was only about ten feet from the shaft. The rocks were different shades of dull gray. I felt the sides of the cave with my hands and announced, "Limestone." My voice echoed off the walls of the cavern.

"No, Runt. It's real, gen-yoo-ine gold," Nathan scoffed.

"Townsfolk," Josie said, shaking his head.

I knew they were just teasing me. I was quickly learning not to get mad when they made fun of me. They did the same with each other—except for Ray. Nobody made fun of Ray. Anyway, I just went along with it. I figured picking on me was their way of letting me know they liked me.

"I hear Pop owns half of the B & O now," Nathan stated. "I heard you guys live in a mansion in Seymour."

I had never thought about it like that before. We did live in a pretty big house, and we did have a maid, but I never thought we were rich. And I was fairly certain Pop didn't *own* the railroad. "Pop's a dispatcher," I clarified.

"Yeah, my dad's a telegraph operator; they work together," Birdy chimed in.

"That's very convenient," Nathan said mockingly as he smirked and looked at everyone else.

"Pop's a dispatcher! I know that for a fact!" I insisted. "I've seen where he works."

Nathan and Josie shot each other a sideways glance and chuckled.

"What they're trying to say is that Pop doesn't do much dispatching anymore and Uncle Walt doesn't do much telegraphing, either. They just walk around telling everybody else what to do," Ray sneered.

When I looked at Birdy, he just shrugged and tilted his head slightly in a way that let me know I should drop it. He and I both knew that older boys could get mean if you sassed them too much. And I didn't want Ray to be mad at me.

Josie attempted to ease the tension by saying, "Our old man says he's sure appreciative of Pop and Uncle Walt for helping him with the side business. He says Pop and Uncle Walt can transport his special deliveries anywhere and guarantee no one will steal them."

It took me a minute to figure out what Josie was talking about. His old man—who I guessed was an uncle of mine that I didn't know—was distilling homemade hooch. It seemed like everybody in Two Counties was making and selling liquor since it had become illegal.

Josie continued on, "He says the railroad is full of thieves and cutthroats."

A chill ran down my spine as I thought of the Giant. I'm sure he would've cut my throat—no doubt about it. The thought of what it might feel like to have my throat cut popped into my head, so I quickly tried to think of something else. I took off my hat and put it down next to me as I wiped my brow, anxious at such a thought.

"What's wrong, Russ?" Birdy asked.

"I think I had a run-in with a cutthroat on the train this morning," I confessed. I hadn't wanted to mention it because the thought of it frightened me, but I blurted it out without thinking. Suddenly, everyone's eyes were on me—even Ray's. It became very quiet as they all waited for me to explain what had happened on the train. As I told the story, I purposely left out a few details . . . like how scared I was. But I did describe what the Giant looked like and what he was wearing—including the Colt and the badge on his belt. When I told them what I'd called him, they all burst out laughing. I even told them that he tried to throw me off the train, but I left out the part about me attempting to train walk. I just told them I was hanging out the window looking at the scenery and enjoying the breeze.

Birdy whistled slowly and remarked, "Woo-wee! It's a good thing Pop showed up when he did!"

"Yeah. . . . The guy sounds like a cutthroat fo' sure!" Nathan said as Josie nodded.

"Nah . . . sounds like a train marshal to me," Ray shot back. "He was probably just tryin' to scare you to keep you from climbin' outta the train."

"That's what Pop said," I admitted with a shrug.

"I don't care what Pop says!" Ray barked with a scowl. It was strange to hear anyone say they didn't want to hear what Pop had to say. It seemed like people were always wanting Pop's opinion on things. *I wonder why Ray said that?*

No one said anything for a while, until finally, Ray broke the silence, "This is boring. Josie, you gonna just sit there and shuck your corn, or are you gonna get me a sip?"

"Right away, sir," Josie said, trying to sound like a waiter on a fancy train. He climbed up the rocks at the back of the cave and put both of his arms into a large hole.

I was curious, so I followed him and peered into the hole; it was pitch-black. *I wonder what's back there?* I thought.

Josie must've read my mind because he said, "If you crawl through this hole, it opens up to a much larger chamber behind these rocks. It's large enough that you could even drive a Fat Angus through there!"

I had no idea who Fat Angus was, but I wondered if he looked like Porky Percy, a kid who lived back home on Fourth Street.

"How far back does it go?" I asked.

"I don't know, miles maybe. It starts to drop down as soon as you get to the other side of the rocks, and you need a light to see. You even have to swim through parts of it. We crawled back there a couple of times, but we didn't go far. I hear it's not as extensive as the caves along the Lost River, but it's deep enough for us. We didn't want to get lost," Josie admitted.

"A couple of kids got lost back there years ago— before we were born—and they never found 'em," Birdy said. "You won't catch me crawlin' back there—no sirree!"

"Rebel Joe killed 'em," Josie said.

Nathan nodded in agreement.

"No, he didn't!" Ray admonished.

I glanced at Ray and he looked back at me then turned his head. I thought Rebel Joe was the hooch, but it sounded like he might be a real person—a horrible person who killed some boys in this cave. That made me a bit more scared than I wanted to be.

Josie climbed back farther into the hole, his legs kicking and sticking out. When he made his way out, he was holding a black bottle with a large cork in it and the initials R. J. on the side.

"Hey! Those are my initials . . . for Russell Joseph!"

"It stands for Rebel Joe," Birdy corrected.

"Oh," I said. That made sense. After all, I figured Rebel Joe was their code name for liquor. *But then who killed the boys?* I wondered. I was really confused.

Josie handed the bottle to Ray, who removed the cork and took a swig. Afterward, he puckered his face, closed his eyes, and shook his head. "There we go," he said hoarsely as if something had burned his throat. Then he sighed deeply, "That gets rid of the boo-boos real quick."

He handed the bottle to Nathan, who coughed a bit after taking a drink. Josie went next. He took a sip then coughed a lot. When he finally stopped, he gave everyone a thumbs-up and handed the bottle to Birdy. Birdy took a sip, but as he did, Nathan gave him a stern warning, "Birdy, I'm telling you, if you throw up again, I'll beat you worse than you beat your cob at night."

As the older fellas laughed, Birdy shook his head violently then took a gulp from the bottle. When he was done, he choked more than Josie did. "No fair making me laugh while I sip," he said, still hacking. Ray laughed longer than I'd seen him laugh all day.

Birdy handed me the bottle and smiled. I didn't want the guys to think I was a little kid, so I held the bottle up to my nose and took a sniff. It smelled harsh and burned my nose, but, at the same time, it smelled familiar. "Hey, this smells like Pop's whiskey glass!"

"Only the best," Nathan said and everyone laughed.

"The trick is not to taste it too much, Russ," Birdy advised. "Just take a sip and swallow it real quick—like medicine."

I nodded. Pretending it was medicine, I put the bottle to my lips, took a mouthful, and swallowed it whole. I immediately regretted it. When I took my first breath, it felt like my lungs were on fire. I began to cough, but that only made my throat burn more. The inside of my nose burned too, which made it hard to breathe. I took a couple more deep breaths and wondered when it would end.

I had no idea alcohol tasted that bad. *How can Pop drink this stuff?* I thought. *How can* anyone *drink this?* I took a few deep breaths then started to breathe normally again. I looked up at the guys, nodded, and gave them a thumbs-up. "Only the best," I managed to croak.

CHAPTER 7

Friday, July 13, 1924, 10:52 a.m.

Two Counties

The guys all laughed at the way I reacted to my first drink of the Rebel Joe. But Birdy patted me on the back, and Ray smiled at me as I handed him the bottle.

I watched as the bottle made its way around the circle. My second sip didn't taste any better than the first, but I didn't cough as much. After a while, my face started to feel numb.

When the bottle came back to me on its next lap, I studied it for a bit. *Rebel Joe and I have the same initials,* I thought. *I wonder if Rebel Joe is a real person? And what does he look like?* Back home, I'd seen a scary painting of a menacing-looking Rebel soldier from the Civil War. He was part of a bayonet charge. I wondered if Rebel Joe looked like that.

"This is the real stuff, not the homemade shit everyone is making now. It's better . . . sweeter. Can you taste that, Ray?" Nathan asked.

Ray nodded.

"Where'd you find it?" Nathan inquired.

73

"Stashed away in one of Ida's closets back home," Ray answered.

"She probably kept it for medicinal purposes. She's good at that stuff, y'know. Now some poor ol' soul won't get his medicine because of you, Ray," Nathan said.

Ray smiled, "It's a good thing I'm not some poor ol' soul then."

I downed my next sip quickly. I must've been getting better at it because I didn't cough that time. After a bit, Ray grabbed the bottle from me.

Suddenly, I was transfixed by the wall of the cave. The light from the shaft below reflected off the water and danced up the sides of the cave. It seemed like the flickering light of the candle and the lights from the shaft were moving in time to the sound of the water trickling from the waterfall below us. My face was still numb, and my head felt lighter. It was a wonderful feeling. I loved me some Rebel Joe.

As I looked at each of the guys, Josie saw me looking at him and gave me a smile and a wink. He looked like he was having fun too. I felt like I was one of the guys. Even though I'd almost died—twice—this was the best day of my entire life!

"You're holding up the line, Russ," Nathan scolded as Birdy tapped the bottle on my arm. I had forgotten to take my turn. Now everyone was laughing at me.

"Hold your horses, Hirdy," I slurred as I yanked the bottle out of Birdy's hands.

All the guys erupted in laughter—even Ray. Birdy did punch me in the arm, but it didn't hurt as much as I thought it would. In fact, it just made me tip over a bit, which only made everyone howl with laughter even more.

I took a swig, made the yucky face at Birdy, then handed Ray the bottle. "Why's it called Rebel Joe?" I asked no one in particular.

"It's named for the guy who first made it. He lived around here back in the olden days. They say he was a no good dirty dog cutthroat Rebel from the Civil War. If he caught you out by yourself, he'd kill you quick. According to stories, he used to live in this cave. Folks say his ghost still haunts the cave and roams Two Counties just like he did when he was alive. They say his ghost wanders around taking revenge on Northerners on account of him being a Rebel and all."

I liked Josie's story, but I didn't believe in ghosts; Pop said they weren't real. Nevertheless, I still enjoyed ghost stories, so I wanted Josie to keep going. "What's Rebel Joe look like?" I asked.

"Well, according to legend, he wears an old gray Confederate uniform and hat and carries his trusty ol' musket. I don't know for sure, though, 'cause I've never seen him."

Ray shook his head and held up his hand to interrupt Josie. Then he looked right at me and clarified,

"He was just a regular ol' guy who made a good whiskey—probably the best. I'm sure he's dead by now. But he did probably make the stuff himself in this here bottle. I don't think he was a real Rebel, though. It was just a catchy name he used to sell his whiskey."

"Iss cootchy . . . I mean, it is catchy," I giggled then burped. Everyone else laughed too.

"He may have even been kin," Ray added with a shrug. "But, then again, almost everyone here in these parts is kin."

"I know people who see him all the time," Nathan chimed in.

"No way! . . . He'd probably be a hundred years old by now!" Josie exclaimed. "Besides, Tom and Andy Riggs said they saw his ghost last fall. They were fishing off the banks of the Lost River when they saw him watching them. He was up on a hill right by the cemetery. Pretty creepy, huh? Tom ran up the hill, but by the time he got there, Rebel Joe had vanished. An old guy can't just run down a hill without being seen, and Tom had a view of the whole valley. You can't tell me that's not a real ghost, Ray. Real people don't just disappear."

"Maybe he's like Crooked Steve, you know, the fella who lives in the woods and looks in windows at night," Nathan said with a smirk. "You know, *girls'* windows . . ."

"Rebel Joe's not like Crooked Steve, and he's not a ghost!" Ray said vehemently. "I'm telling you, he was just a man who knew how to make some damn good hooch with a catchy name for it. Anyway, he's dead now, so he can't be at the top of any hill."

"But Tom and Andy are really into Bible learnin'!" Josie defended his argument. "They even volunteer at church, so they don't seem like the type to lie or make stuff up."

Ray was hot under the collar all of a sudden. "Yeah, they *do* seem like the type to make stuff up. Church is a con—it's the oldest con in the book! How can it not be if you have to fool yourself into believing that a man in the sky watches you shuck your corn every night, Josie? You can believe in your con god for all I care. I personally don't give a shit! But if you believe in it, you're a jack, Josie. There's no such thing as ghosts; there's no such thing as Crooked Steve; and there's no such thing as God!"

"Good lord, Ray. God's gonna make the walls of this cave come crashin' down on us for that outburst, . . . I just know it," Josie said, completely serious. He looked at his brother, but Nathan just shrugged.

In a flash, Ray leaped up, landed right in front of Josie, and yelled, "Oh my God! Rebel Joe is right behind you!"

Josie screamed like a baby—twice, but then his expression turned angry. "Damn you, Ray! I wasn't scared!"

I glanced over at Nathan, who was doubled over laughing. I turned to see Birdy giggling with his hands over his mouth. It was almost like I was at the picture show watching a scary movie—but with sound. Ray had scared the crap out of me, but he was hilarious. Josie wasn't laughing, though. He was still too angry ... and probably scared as well, although he would never admit it.

Ray wasn't laughing, either. He scowled at Josie, shoved the bottle at him, then turned and climbed down the shaft. I figured Ray was right about religion. Pop didn't take to no Bible learnin'; in fact, he and I never talked about the Bible at all—except around Christmas and Easter, of course. Mom used to take me to church with her when I was younger, but she only went to play the organ and then played cards with her friends. It was boring. After a while, I just pretended to be asleep when she left so I didn't have to go with her.

"I believe in God," Nathan confessed. "But I don't believe in the ghost of Rebel Joe. And I think Crooked Steve could be a real guy, not a phantom like Rebel Joe. There are just too many stories about him peeking into windows at night, especially to look at naked girls," Nathan said with a wink.

"I think you should be called Crooked Nathan for all the peeping you do," Josie joked as he walked to the back of the cave, wiggled into the hole, and stuck the bottle back where he'd gotten it earlier.

"Are we done? I won s'more," I slurred.

"Look ... Russ is drunk," Birdy giggled, pointing at me. Nathan and Josie did the same. I did want another drink, though. Didn't everyone?

"If you don't throw up like Birdy did last time, we can come back later. There's plenty," Nathan promised.

That sounded terrific! I couldn't wait 'til later. I also wanted to talk more with Ray. There was so much I didn't know about him, and I had a million questions. It was hard for me to believe that he was my brother and I'd just met him. And I wasn't scared of him anymore, I liked him. I wondered if he could come live with us. That would be the best thing ever.

I got up and climbed back down the shaft. While no one was looking, I took another drink at the waterfall to get the Rebel Joe taste out of my mouth.

As I moved from rock to rock toward the front of the cave, little crawdads darted here and there in the water. When I made it to the entrance, I remembered to duck my head so I didn't bump it on the top of the cave. I could still hear Josie and Nathan deliberating the existence of Rebel Joe and Crooked Steve from deep inside the cave.

The sun flashed in my eyes as I stepped outside. It was so bright I couldn't even keep both my eyes open. As I blinked my eyes, I noticed Ray leaning against a tree, smoking a cigarette. He glanced over at me then purposely looked away. I walked over and tried to stand just like he did, with one leg bent at the knee and my foot resting against the tree. It was hard to keep my balance, but I stood there for a minute or two and didn't say anything. Ray ignored me the whole time.

"Hey, Ray," I said casually.

He glared at me like I had five eyeballs and arms growing out of my ears. Then he did a double take and asked, "Where's your hat?"

"Oh," I said, feeling the top of my head. "I guess I left it in the cave."

"Well, you better go back and get it."

"I'm no jack, Ray. I dun't b'leave in any of that schtuff, either. I jus won you to know," I said.

Ray continued to ignore me.

"Ray, can I aks you a question?"

"No," he grumbled.

"Why dun't choo live with us?" I asked anyway.

For a brief second, Ray looked at me differently. For the first time since I'd met him, he looked scared. Then his expression turned menacing, and he looked away. He sighed deeply and started to say something but then stopped. He looked back at me and smirked, "Because Pop doesn't want me around, kid."

I stared at him in disbelief. *How could Pop not want Ray?* I thought. *Pop loves everybody!* It didn't make any sense. It couldn't be true. "No way, Ray! Pop . . ." was all I could get out. I couldn't think of what else to say. I was still trying to process Ray's answer to my question.

"Listen, kid. You're alright . . . sorta . . . so don't go meddling. Pop never wanted me. Let's just leave it at that." Ray shook his head, "He's the worst father in Two Counties."

"You're a liar!" I shouted. I stepped in front of Ray and clenched my fists. "You dun't know nothin' 'bout Pop! He's a good guy and the bess father anyone could aks for!" I was angry, and I didn't even really know why. I unclenched my fists, but I couldn't calm down.

Ray just stared at me as I stood my ground. "Just drop it, kid," he ordered.

"Maybe I could talk to him?" I offered.

"Maybe you could, but that whore mother of yours would never let me near your damn Seymour mansion." Ray bent down and whispered to me low, "During the war, she let all the Huns in Huntington hump her, you know, for the Kaiser and all."

I got mad somethin' severe. "You better take that back, or I'll beat you good!" I shouted. I pushed Ray with both hands, but he didn't even budge. He just looked at me smugly. Then he pushed me hard enough with one hand that I fell to the ground and landed on my butt. I was fuming mad, and suddenly, I hated Ray. I was so angry that I wanted to bite the hand he pushed me with.

"Hey, Russ! Why don't you come back over here?" Birdy yelled from behind me. I turned and noticed the guys watching Ray and me from the entrance to the cave. Nathan was putting the fence post with the barbed wire back into place. Josie smiled, nodded, and motioned for me to come back too.

"No!" I spat. I couldn't think of anything else to say. So I turned to Ray and in my meanest voice, I lied like I'd never lied before, "Pop *does* hate you! He told me so! He told everyone!"

Mom said I had a temper. I didn't know why I said it, but I didn't have time to think about it. I saw a blur of motion out of the corner of my eye. And by the time I saw Ray's fist, it was barreling into my stomach. The force of the punch knocked the wind out of me and sent me sailing through the air. I saw the sky as I fell backward and bounced off the ground. When I opened my eyes, I figured Ray would pounce on me to finish me off, but he didn't. He just turned and walked away.

I couldn't breathe. As I lay there trying to catch my breath, Nathan came over, looked down at me, and hissed, "Dumbass."

Then Josie walked by and just shook his head. "Why'd ya have to start a fight, Russ? Everybody was having a good time."

They both left me there and followed Ray. Birdy sat down beside me on the ground as I mouthed, "I can't breathe."

"Juss relask and take little brefs," he said with a slur.

I did what he said, and after a while, I was able to take some shallow breaths. I moaned and kept trying to relax and catch my breath.

"Damn, Russ! You're a mean drunk, ain't ya?" Birdy hooted.

I was still mad enough to cry, but I stopped myself. "He coulda killed me! I couldn't breathe!" I sputtered.

"You can't die from getting the wind knocked out of you, Russ," Birdy scolded. "So stop actin' like a baby."

That might've been true, but I still *felt* like I was dying.

Birdy looked down at me with a scared look in his eyes. "My mom told me once thass what it feels like when you're dyin', though. It feels like your wind's all gone. Iss scary."

I just lay there and nodded my head. It hurt too much to talk.

Birdy shook his head. "Damn, Russ. You told him Pop hated him. That was really mean. Boy, oh boy, you were aksin' for it! *Pow!* It looked like it hurt somethin' awful, though."

It had hurt something awful. And I didn't want to think about it or talk about it anymore. As I took a closer look at Birdy, he didn't look so good, either. He looked a little green around the gills.

"Hey, Russ," he confided, "before we left, I aksed my mom why you've never met Ray. She says iss 'cause you and Ray have different mothers. My Auntie Edna is *your* mom, but she ain't Ray's mom. Thass why Ray lives with Ida, I guess."

I sat up and looked at Birdy as I tried to process this confusing information. And there was that name again. Ida. It had never occurred to me that brothers could have different moms.

"You can't tell Pop I told you this, and you can't tell him you and Ray got in a fight," Birdy insisted. "Ray could get in big trouble."

I nodded. I didn't want to tell anyone anything. In fact, I hoped I never had to think about it again. I also hoped no one would ever find out about me getting whopped. "Do you think Nathan and Josie will tell anyone?"

"Juss every kid in Two Counties!" Birdy laughed. "But they won't tell any adults, thass fo' sure."

"You said Ray lives with Ida. But who's Ida?"

"Shut up," Birdy said, cracking a smile. He laughed and then did a double take when he realized I wasn't kidding. "Damn, Russ! You don't know who Ida is?"

I shook my head.

"She's my grandma. Heck, she's *your* grandma— my dad's mom—Pop's mom! Doesn't Pop tell you anything? This is like the weirdest thing I've ever heard in my life," Birdy groaned. He lay down on the grass and put his forearm over his eyes to block the sun.

I took a deep breath and sighed. I knew a couple of kids back home who lived with their grandparents, so I could make sense of that. As I sat there, the ground began to sway to the left as if it were going to come up and smack me in the face. I felt like I was on the train again—or a boat on a choppy sea. Then I remembered Ray bragging about driving Grandpa Marker's car. "Is she Grandma Marker?" I asked.

"Yes. . . . No. . . . Yes," Birdy wavered. "Uh, iss confusing. She's Grandma Marker now, but we don't call her that; we call her Ida. She married a guy named Marker who's a millionaire up in Minnesota."

"Got it," I said, even though I didn't. I had no clue what Birdy was talking about. As I attempted to stand up, the ground started to roll again. I tried not to fall over, but I failed miserably. Birdy laughed at me and helped me up, but then he fell and took me down with him. We both reclined on the ground and laughed for a bit. I looked around at the trees and the hills before trying to stand again. This time, Two Counties had stopped moving—at least for the time being.

I jumped as a voice came from the woods. "C'mon, ya stinkin' runts! We're going to the pond!" Nathan yelled from up ahead. "If ya don't come now, we're leavin' ya!"

Birdy rolled over onto his belly, kneeled on all fours, then stood up shakily. "We're comin'!" he shouted back.

As Birdy started to walk toward the tree line, he stopped and looked back at me. "C'mon, Russ. Don't be a baby. Ray won't hit ya again, I promise. He's not a bad guy. He'll leave ya alone as long as ya don't start anything with him . . . promise."

I didn't know what to do. I was hot and sweaty, so the pond sounded like fun. But I kinda wanted to be alone. My feelings about Ray and Pop were all mixed up.

"Go on ahead, Birdy. I'm gonna go to the rope for a while."

"C'mon, Russ! Iss the pond!" Birdy implored me. "Usually around this time, the Burton girls come for a swim. Some of them are older girls, too, Russ! They skinny-dip, and we do too. You can see their boobies, Russ!" He had a goofy grin on his face and was bouncing at double his normal rate.

"But I dun't want girls to see me naked!" I said.

"You're silly, everybody's naked, so it doesn't matter."

It mattered to me. I shook my head until Birdy gave up trying to convince me.

"Suit yourself, Russ. The pond is a five-minute walk from here," he said, pointing toward the woods. "We'll come by the rope on the way back, so stay there."

"OK, Birdy. Go to the pond and come back and get me after you swim naked. Make sure you dress yourself before you come back."

"Wash ou' for Rebel Joe," Birdy laughed as he bounded off for the tree line. He fell about halfway there, but quickly got back on his feet, gave me a thumbs-up, and ran into the woods.

Chapter 8

I was still a little woozy, so when I stood up, I fell back down a couple of times. I'd seen Pop drunk before, so I knew I was too. I laughed at myself and walked toward the Grand Chasm. I found the path pretty easily and followed the sound of the water toward the stream. But this time, the stream sounded louder and appeared darker.

The rope was hanging over the middle of the Grand Chasm, so I couldn't reach it, and I couldn't ask anyone for help. I studied the rope and the ravine, trying to figure out how I could get ahold of the rope. Then, remembering what Ray had done, I decided to try to jump out and grab the rope then swing back and forth until I got enough height.

I figured I could do it, so I gave myself enough distance to gain speed, then I took off running toward the ravine as fast as I could, even though a voice inside my head told me not to. As the Grand Chasm came closer, I started to doubt whether I could make it, so I put on the brakes just before I reached the edge. Instead, I tripped and tumbled down the side of the ravine and landed in the stream.

It didn't hurt too much; although for a moment, I was scared that I might drown. But once I stood up, I realized the stream only came up to my knees.

Climbing out of the Grand Chasm was more difficult than I thought it would be, though. The sides were steep, and it was hard to climb to the top. Plus, I was soaking wet. *This has been the worst day of my life.*

When I finally made it to the top, I began walking in the direction of the pond. I was drenched from head to toe, and my boots made sloshing sounds when I walked. Birdy had said the pond was nearby, so I figured I'd just go swim with the guys and let my clothes dry at the same time. I'd also apologize to Ray. They'd probably tease me for falling down the ravine and getting all wet, but I didn't care; it would still be fun.

The sun was warm on my head, and as I looked up at the sky, I became dizzy and fell. When I got up, I looked at the sky one more time, and my head started spinning again, so I decided to stop doing that. I retraced my steps back to the cave.

I had just descended into the bubbly brook when I saw him. He was standing at the mouth of the cave looking at the barbed wire. He must have heard me because he turned around quick and saw me. He had a bristly beard and looked ancient. He wore a gray uniform and a gray hat and held a musket in his hands. A cold chill went down my back, when I realized, *Oh my god! That's Rebel Joe!*

I screamed like a baby as I turned and ran from the cave as fast as possible. I didn't look back—I just wanted to get away as fast as I could. When I made it to the woods, I found the path to the rope again and ran toward the Grand Chasm in record time. As I ran, I figured I'd have to swing across the ravine to get to the other side fast enough so that I didn't get caught by the murderous ghost. So I kept running at the ravine at full speed. I promised myself I wouldn't stop this time, and before I could talk myself out of it, I was jumping through the air over the Grand Chasm watching the water rush below me. I surprised myself by not only reaching the rope this time but holding on! My momentum easily carried me across the ravine, but I forgot to climb the rope, so I slammed into the other side of the Grand Chasm. I almost fell backward into the stream, but I grabbed ahold of some weeds, roots, and whatever else I could find to steady myself, then I quickly climbed to the top of the slope.

I took a second to catch my breath and realized that I'd seen the ghost of Rebel Joe! And I didn't want him to kill me for being a Northerner or for trespassing in his cave. Suddenly, I missed Mom something awful and couldn't wait to see her again. But to do that, I knew that I first needed to get back to town. I couldn't meet the guys on the other side of the ravine as planned because Rebel Joe was over there. And I was not going anywhere near him if I could help it!

So I took off for town. I still didn't look back. As I ran, one side of my brain tried to reason with the other side. "Ghosts aren't real," the one side said. "He looked real enough to kill me!" the other side countered.

To make matters worse, I kept seeing the ghost of Rebel Joe in my mind: his face, his hat, his musket. He looked like the oldest man in the world, only older. And just like that, I became a believer in ghosts.

I ran a good distance along the path, but nothing looked familiar. I couldn't find the meadow with cow pies where I'd been shot at earlier. But I kept running anyway. I only slowed down when I saw bright sunlight shining down on the path as the trees began to open up. I stopped and took a couple of tentative steps forward to see what was ahead. I was filled with joy and relief when I saw railroad tracks. I sprinted the last few yards, and in no time, I was standing in the middle of the tracks.

I was fairly sure these were the same railroad tracks we'd followed west out of town on our way to Rebel Joe's cave. If so, all I had to do was turn right and follow the tracks east into town. But nothing looked familiar, and my mind started playing tricks on me. I had lost my sense of direction. Then I started second-guessing myself, figuring that I might've run so far east that I was actually at the tracks running south out of town. And if that was the case, then I needed to turn left and follow the tracks north into town. Rebel Joe—both the hooch and the ghost—had made it hard for me to make up my mind.

The path in front of me was well worn and easy to see. But no matter what side of town I was on, that path wouldn't lead me anywhere, I figured. I looked to the left and then to the right. And then I had a brilliant idea. All I had to do was sit down in the shade, take a nice break, and wait for the next train to steam by. If it was the B & O, then I'd turn right, and if it was a Monon, I'd turn left. That would solve the conundrum. Plus, with all the running I'd done, sitting down in the shade and relaxing sounded like the best plan of all. But I'd forgotten for a moment why I'd been running in the first place: I was trying to escape the ghost of Rebel Joe. That's when I remembered I hadn't looked behind me in quite some time.

I slowly turned around to see Rebel Joe standing behind me at the edge of the woods. He was staring at me with his deadly dark eyes. He didn't seem real, but the rifle in his hand looked real enough. I screamed louder than before. When I did, Rebel Joe's eyes got big and mean, and he scowled and raised his rifle. That was all I saw before I turned and took off down the path in front of me.

I ran for what seemed like hours, but it probably wasn't nearly that long. I finally stopped to catch my breath when the path widened and turned into a dirt road. I looked back regularly after that, but I didn't hear or see Rebel Joe following me. I wondered if maybe ghosts couldn't cross railroad tracks, but I figured I'd better not count on it. I looked around for anything familiar, but I still didn't recognize anything, so I kept walking until I came to a cornfield. I made my way along the edge of the cornfield for a while and followed another dirt road. At that point, I realized I was lost and nearly cried. I admitted to myself that I should've gone to the pond with the guys—and I shouldn't have started a fight with Ray. I decided it was best to keep walking and find someone—anyone alive—who could help me.

As I ambled along, I passed two more cornfields and two farmhouses. I spied on the farmhouses from a distance but didn't see anyone around, and when I heard dogs barking, I ran. I was afraid to get bitten, so I steered clear of farmhouses after that.

After a while, I came to a large grassy field with a single tree in the middle of it. I walked over and stood in the shade beneath the tree, hoping to cool off a bit. The long tallgrass billowed in the breeze, giving it the appearance of waves crashing along a shore.

Up ahead, I noticed a soaring tree-covered hill that blocked a good portion of the horizon. It was the largest hill I'd seen all day, so I named it Mount R. J., after me, of course.

"Help!" I screamed as loud as I could. A few seconds later, my voice echoed back from Mount R. J. I waited for a moment and cried out, "Somebody help me!" But the only response I got came from Mount R. J. Dejected, I plopped down in the shade and stared up at the trees on the hill, trying to figure out what to do next.

When my head started to spin again, I lay down on my back and looked up at the sky. It was a deep cerulean blue with puffy white clouds scattered about. I closed my eyes for a while, and when I opened them, Rebel Joe was staring down at me through the barrel of his rifle.

I sat up in such a hurry that I got muddled really bad and almost fell back down. I was able to steady myself, but I was so scared I didn't know what to do. I sat there frozen, unable to talk or yell or cry or holler. I wondered how long it would take for him to kill me.

"Pop, is that you?" Rebel Joe asked tentatively. His voice sounded gravelly and old yet vaguely familiar.

We just stared at each other for a while as I tried to relax and figure out what to do. *Why the hell did he call me Pop?* I wondered.

"Maybe I shoulda shot you back there instead of chasing you all the way here!" he growled.

"No, please!" I begged as I put my hands up to shield myself from the rifle. "I'm not Pop; I'm his son. Pop's my daddy!"

Rebel Joe took a step back. He put down his rifle and leaned against it with a confused look on his face. Then he smiled. He had a scary smile because he was missing several teeth. "Ah, I see. You must be Pop Jr."

I thought for a second. No one had ever called me that before, but Rebel Joe was right. Pop and I were both named Russell, so technically, I was Pop Jr.

"Yes! I *am* Pop Jr.!"

"That's sure a good thing," he chuckled, pointing down at me. "I thought you were a ghost!"

"I thought *you* were a ghost!" I laughed back.

Rebel Joe gave me a toothless grin and shook his head. "That makes us a sorry pair, don't it?"

"I guess so!" I agreed and smiled, but I was still scared of him since he was holding his gun. Plus, he was a mountain of a man up close, and he blocked my view of Mount R. J. He wasn't as big as the Giant, but he wasn't too far off, either.

"Who put the barbed wire over the cave?" he questioned me.

95

"Uncle Isom," I replied.

"Which one?" he inquired.

I shrugged.

"So what are you doing out this way, Pop Jr.?" he asked.

"I'm headed back to town, but I think I'm lost," I admitted.

He paused for a moment, perhaps considering what I'd said. He looked in the direction from where I'd come, then he looked up at the sky. Finally, he looked at me and said, "Where's your hat, boy?"

"I lost it," I confessed.

"You ought not do that," he said. Which sounded familiar to me because Pop said it to me too. "Well, let's go, then."

"Yes, sir," I replied. "So where are we going?"

"I thought you needed help getting back to town," he grumbled as he headed off toward Mount R. J.

I followed behind, even though I still wasn't too sure about him. He seemed too real to be a ghost, and he was nice to me once he knew who I was. He was a bit confused, though, that was for sure. But he was my only chance at getting back to town. So I figured I could follow Rebel Joe or stay lost, and I was tired of being lost.

As we strolled through a field, bugs buzzed and birds chirped a million songs. I didn't know what to say, so I stayed quiet. But I was really curious how he knew Pop, so after a while, I asked him, "How do you know Pop?"

He turned around and gave me a toothless grin. "Oh, Pop and I were good buddies a long time ago. I knew him when he was your age. We used to talk about everything. I sure do miss those days," he said, looking a little sad. "He even taught me how to do this." Rebel Joe put his finger in his mouth and pulled. *Pop!*

When I popped too, Rebel Joe laughed.

"Pop really taught you how to pop?" I asked. "You're not joking, are you?"

"Honest truth," he said. Then he paused for a moment before continuing, "Anyway, we best keep movin'."

As we started walking again, I remembered something Josie had said and wondered what the old man would say. "You ever been down to the Lost River?"

"Oh, sure. I was born not too far from it. A lot of your kin were too," he replied.

As we got closer to Mount R. J., it looked even taller than before. "We're not going to climb that hill are we, sir?" I asked.

"Yep. That's the fastest way to get you back to town," he said. "Don't worry. I know a path that's not too hard to climb."

"I named it Mount R. J. when I first saw it."

He looked at me and smiled, "Oh, ya did, huh?... I called it something different in my day."

We made our way out of the field and began to follow a path in the woods. The farther we walked, the more arduous it became. The forest was dense, and I could only see a few feet in front of me. I did my best to keep up with Rebel Joe, who just kept walking up the hill higher and higher.

As the path became steeper, Rebel Joe grabbed onto roots and branches to help him climb, but he didn't seem tired. I sure was, though! I grabbed the same roots and branches he did as we continued our ascent up the hill. I fell behind a couple times, but he didn't get mad; he just waited patiently for me and encouraged, "Come on, Pop Jr.! You can do it!"

After a while, the ground evened out, the path disappeared, and the walk became easier. At the top of the hill, we came to a small meadow surrounded by trees and filled with wildflowers of all colors.

All of a sudden, I saw it as we left the woods. It took my breath away, and I couldn't talk for a moment. It looked exactly like the giant aliens in the illustrations in *War of the Worlds*. The metal structure reached up into the sky, and the wires coming down from it made it look like an enormous steel insect more than a martian. After a second, I recognized what it was, but still, gaping up at it, I got vertigo so bad I nearly fell over.

"Whoa!" I gasped, steadying myself.

"Exactly," Rebel Joe said nodding his head. "What is it, Pop?"

"Pop Jr.," I corrected him.

"Pop Jr.," he acknowledged.

I stopped staring up so I wouldn't fall over and turned to Rebel Joe, "It's a radio tower. They've been putting 'em up all along the railroad lately. Pop said two of 'em already fell down 'cause of storms."

"A radio tower, eh? Did Pop build it?" Rebel Joe asked, looking confused.

"From what I heard today, Pop doesn't really do things, he tells other people to do things. Does that make sense?" I asked.

"Sure does! Pop's the boss, now," Rebel Joe stated.

I shrugged as a flock of birds flew overhead and landed on the tower.

Rebel Joe took a seat on a stump and smiled at me. I was getting used to his smile, but I hoped I didn't lose any teeth like him when I was older.

I didn't want to seem impolite, but I was starting to wonder if he'd forgotten that he was going to show me how to get to town, so I asked politely, "Sir, can you show me how to get to town now?"

"I can and I will. But you know, you can get there on your own from here if you just head in the right direction," he said.

"But I don't know where I am," I replied, figuring Rebel Joe was confused again.

"Climb up that there thing to the first platform, and you'll see it . . . you'll see where you're headin'," he said pointing at the radio tower.

"Really? Can I?" I asked.

"I don't know, can ya?" Rebel Joe joked back.

I didn't wait for him to change his mind. I bounded off toward the radio tower at top speed. When I got to the tower, I noticed a ladder going all the way up to the top, so I started to climb. It was pretty easy—so easy a five-year-old could probably climb it. For a moment, I worried that the tower might fall over. Pop had told me about that happening before. But then I remembered those had fallen over during a storm, so I began to climb. Every now and then, I looked back to check on Rebel Joe. Every time I looked, he was watching me and gave me a wave. With a big smile, I climbed up into the sky. Soon enough, I was higher than all of the trees. Finally, after quite a bit of climbing, I made it to the first platform.

The whole wide world surrounded me. And I could see for miles, maybe more. From horizon to horizon, Two Counties was an endless rolling sea of green trees and hills going on forever. I just stood there in the sky and admired the vista. There was a nice cool breeze, too, which felt refreshing after walking for so long in the heat. I couldn't remember ever being up so high in all my life.

Rebel Joe hollered from below as he pointed off to the east, "Look out thataway."

I did as he instructed and turned around so I could see where he was pointing. As I scanned the horizon, the view didn't seem much different than before. But then I saw what he wanted me to see. "I see it! I see it!" I yelled.

Sticking right out between the trees below me was a water tower with the word "Mitchell" painted on the side of it.

"You're the tallest man in Two Counties now!" Rebel Joe shouted.

"Woo-hoo!" I hooted as loud as I could.

I was starting to like the old man. He probably wasn't the real Rebel Joe, but I figured he resembled what the real Rebel Joe looked like, so he was still Rebel Joe to me.

I couldn't wait to tell Birdy about the radio tower and Rebel Joe. I took my time taking in the sights as I climbed down the ladder. It was easier getting down than it was getting up. When I got to the ground, I ran back to Rebel Joe and perched next to him on the stump. It was then that I noticed his rifle was the cleanest part about him. It sparkled in the sun. "What kind of rifle is that?" I asked.

Rebel Joe looked down at it. "Winchester Model 94," he answered. The name sounded familiar to me, but I wasn't sure why.

"Can I shoot it?" I asked.

"No," he chuckled. "Something this big will knock your arm out of its socket. You should start with a .22 'til you get good at it and then come see me."

"Pop won't buy me a .22," I said dejectedly.

"Then buy it yourself," Rebel Joe growled.

"That's a good idea," I said. I'd have to save up some money somehow. I turned to take in the top of the hill. "You know this place well, don't you, sir?"

The old man laughed and said, "Oh, yeah. I was born in Two Counties and have lived in these parts my whole life. But I've walked as far north as Bloomington. You still got kin up that way, y'know." He seemed to think for a minute before continuing, "When I was a young man, I used to ride the flatboats south down the East Fork. That was before the railroads took over. I sailed a few times down to Petersburg and even Mount Carmel."

"Pop and I go fishing in the East Fork," I interjected.

Rebel Joe nodded and continued, "One time I took a steamboat down the Mississippi on the way to Memphis. Never made it."

"Uh, sir," I interrupted. I was trying to be polite, but I didn't want to listen to any boring stories about the old times. I wanted to get back to town as soon as possible.

Rebel Joe glared at me. I guess I hadn't been as polite as I wanted to be.

"Anyway," he said. "Take some advice from an old-timer like me: Never hire on to a steamer heading down the Mississippi with anyone named Crooked Steve. Nothing good can happen after that."

I turned and gave Rebel Joe a wide-eyed look. "I've heard of him," I whispered for no particular reason. "I hear he likes to peep in girls' windows."

Rebel Joe just chuckled and nodded knowingly. But then he went silent for a bit. He just stared at the radio tower. I kept quiet too. When I remembered more of what Josie had said, I finally got up the courage to ask him the question I'd been wondering the whole time. "Were you a Rebel?" I whispered.

He stared at me with his dark eyes. I held my breath. "I recon I killed more northerners," Rebel Joe replied, so quietly I could barely hear him. "But I killed me some southern boys too." And then he turned his gaze back toward the radio tower.

I didn't believe him for a minute. That was against the rules, even I knew that. I figured he hadn't meant to lie to me, but he just was confused again. And I wondered if I might have to help *him* home. His face looked peaceful though, as he stared up at the tower. His mouth moved a bit like he was talking, but no sound came out. It was the same thing Pop did when he was thinking. Scanning the tree line, I quickly found the path that led downhill. I started to deliberate heading back to town on my own since I knew exactly which way it was now. I'd just leave the old codger behind and nobody would be the wiser. But then I figured that would be impolite.

When I glanced back over to Rebel Joe, he had vanished. The stump was empty, and I was by myself. I didn't hear anything except a light breeze humming in my ear. I turned around and the old man was standing right behind me. I almost jumped out of my boots!

"Who the hell are you?" he growled. He was holding his rifle again, but he wasn't pointing it at me yet.

"Remember . . . ?" was all I got out as he backed up, still leering at me.

I got muddled and almost fell down. I had to think clearer. Rebel Joe had forgotten who I was again, and he wasn't joking around—he was crazy!

"I'm Pop Jr.," I reminded him. He was scaring me, and I was starting to get mad at him.

Rebel Joe looked at me angrily for a bit. Then he put his head down and turned around. I heard him sigh.

I took a couple deep breaths and then a couple more. I just stood there for a moment wondering if I should run the other way. But then it occurred to me that running hadn't done me any good so far, so I waited him out.

After a bit, he started walking away from the crest of the hill. "Goin' down's the easy part, Pop," he said.

I finally lost my disposition. Mom said I had a temper. "I'm Pop Jr.!" I yelled. "Damn you, Rebel Joe!"

And then I wished I hadn't said any of it. Damn was a cussword and he was an adult. And calling someone Rebel Joe around these parts was probably just as bad as saying a cussword. I held my breath and waited for him to turn around and shoot me dead.

But he didn't even stop or turn around. He just chuckled a bit and grumbled, "Don't call me that, boy."

Joe, 1864

CHAPTER 9

A s Rebel Joe and I made our way down the winding trail and through the woods, I followed as best I could. For an old guy, he moved pretty quickly, so every now and then, I fell behind. But when I did, he always stopped and waited for me. It was scary when he forgot who I was, so I hoped it wouldn't happen again. I tried to remember everything about the way we were heading so I could lead Birdy back here later.

Rebel Joe was a sight. He had long, gray hair that hung down below his hat, and he *was* wearing an old gray suit that had seen better days—but it wasn't a Confederate uniform like Josie had said. He didn't carry an old-time musket, either. In fact, his rifle looked pretty new to me. I laughed at myself a little for thinking he might be a ghost.

After a while, when the ground flattened out and the woods became less dense, I was able to see three farmhouses through the trees. We walked on a path alongside a small crick that made a pleasant sound as it rolled over the rocks. The sound reminded me of the brook inside the cave. We came to another path that ran toward the house farthest to our left. We followed a new path 'til we came to a fence, which, despite his age, Rebel Joe hopped over pretty easily. After I made my way over it, I noticed the small farmhouse more clearly. I hoped the people who lived there were home so I could ditch

Rebel Joe. I was tired and thirsty, and I just wanted to get back to Uncle Walt's.

I followed Rebel Joe to the end of the path, where a grove of trees butted up against the back of the house. When we got to the trees, he stopped suddenly, smiled his toothless grin, and pointed to an opening between the branches. I peered through the opening and saw the little house up close.

The back of the farmhouse looked newer than the others I'd seen earlier. It had a long porch that looked like it might wrap around the entire house. A swing hung down from the top of the porch. It was long enough that four kids could easily sit on it. I also noticed a little girl who was wearing a blue dress and a matching bonnet. She was maybe Betty's age, and she was talking to a woman whose back was to me. The little girl and the woman were walking down one row of a garden just off the back porch. I heard the little girl giggle and then saw her run into the house. I looked up at Rebel Joe, but he didn't say anything; he just kept staring at the lady. I hoped someone there knew Pop or Uncle Walt or could at least point me in the direction of town. I'd gotten a bit turned around on the way down the hill, so I was no longer sure which way town was.

The garden was long and narrow with several types of flowers growing in it. Some were blue, some were pink, some were yellow, and there were other plants I didn't recognize at all. None of the plants were big yet, but the garden was well tended. The woman seemed to be studying a row of plants. She still had her back to me, so I strained my eyes to see if I recognized her.

When the woman turned around, I noticed she was wearing a colorful dress. Her chestnut brown hair, which was twisted into a bun on top of her head, shined in the bright sun. She was slender like Mom. I couldn't stop staring at her—she was the most elegant woman I'd ever seen. She turned her head, looked up at the sky, and smiled briefly. When she smiled, her whole face lit up. I'd never seen anyone like her before.

I looked back up at the old man and whispered, "She's very pretty."

"Yes, she is," Rebel Joe agreed. But his smile had turned to a look of sadness.

"Who is she?" I whispered.

Rebel Joe looked at me strange, as if I'd said something wrong. He frowned, glanced back at the woman, and then looked at me again, "That's your momma, silly," he answered. "You might need glasses, Pop."

At first, I was mad that he thought I was Pop again, but then I remembered that Pop's momma would be my grandma. And then I wasn't mad, I was stunned. I turned back to get a better look at her face. She was beautiful. I didn't know whether or not to believe Rebel Joe. "That's Ida?" I asked, still whispering.

Rebel Joe nodded, but I thought he might be confused again. I peered at her once more and shook my head—she didn't look old enough to be a grandmother.

So that's Pop's mom, I thought. Until this morning, I didn't even know I had a grandma, and she certainly didn't look like the other kids' grandmas back home.

I wondered again why Mom and Pop hadn't told me about her. And I thought about Mom at home again and felt sad. I would've given just about anything to be home then—not somewhere in Two Counties with an old man who thought I was Pop. When I glanced back at him, he winked at me.

"Alright, we better get going," he said, motioning for me to go in front of him.

As I came out from the cover of the trees, I walked toward the lady with my hand shading my eyes from the bright sunshine. She appeared radiant in the sunlight. I slowed down so as not to startle her. She made me think of home and Mom. The events of this day had been too much for me. I'd been so sad since Ray punched me, and I just wanted to see Pop again. This had been the worst day of my life. Finally, I couldn't stop myself and started to cry. Young men weren't supposed to cry, so I tried to hold it in, but I couldn't help it. Even worse, it came out with a loud yelp.

The woman turned when she realized I was there. She looked at me for a moment and frowned, then she dropped to her knees and held out her arms. I walked over to her and hugged her, crying all the way.

The woman gave me a big hug and didn't let go. I, too, held on tight, clinging to her for what seemed like a day and a half. She held me until I calmed down.

"I'm Ida," she said, wiping the tears from my cheeks and brushing a stray hair from my brow. Her big eyes glistened. "And I am so happy to see you, Russ."

"You know me?" I asked.

Ida giggled. "Of course, I do! I was there when you were born, silly. I delivered you—a perfect baby boy. I was the first person you saw when you opened your eyes to the world."

"I don't remember that," I said.

She giggled again and said, "No, well, I don't suppose you do."

Ida wore makeup and perfume, like Mom did sometimes, as well as a necklace and rings on her fingers. Her voice was so gentle that I gave her another hug.

"There, there," she said, patting my back. "Did you get lost?"

I nodded.

"Well, everything is OK now. I'll take care of you until we get you back to Pop. Whaddaya say?"

I nodded again.

"Russ, I've wanted to spend time with you for so long, and now I get to. That makes me very happy," she said. Ida's voice was soft and magical, not like Mom's. Even when Mom whispered, you could hear her in the next town over. I figured I could listen to Ida say just about anything and enjoy it. She kissed my cheek and forehead. Then she hugged me again before leaning back to look at me. "You look like your father's twin at his age!"

When she said that, I remembered Rebel Joe. But when I turned around, he was gone. He had vanished!

"What's wrong, Russ?" Ida asked. "Did you see something?" She looked out toward the grove of trees.

I looked around for a bit and then replied, "I met an old man. He led me here, but now he's gone."

Ida looked at me confused. After a moment, she said, "An old man, you say?" The way she said it, it sounded like she didn't believe me. She frowned and looked toward the trees again.

When I looked up at her, I felt woozy again. I started to wonder if I'd just imagined him. But then Ida got a big smile on her face as she whispered in my ear, "Maybe it was Rebel Joe."

I gazed into her eyes, wondering how she could've known. *Are grandmas able to read minds?* I wondered. But then it dawned on me that she was probably talking about the ghost stories Josie had been telling. I figured the ghost of Rebel Joe was quite popular around these parts.

"No, ma'am. I don't believe in ghosts," I said.

Ida cackled at that. Her laugh made me smile. "You stay close to me, Russ—just in case. Will you protect me?" She sounded all dramatic like Mom talked sometimes. She grabbed my hand, stood up, and led me out of the garden. I wanted to ask her about Pop, but before I could, she hollered, "Millie! Come quick! We've got a visitor!"

Ida looked down and winked at me, then she pulled out a handkerchief and wiped more tears from my face. The little girl I'd seen earlier came bounding out of the farmhouse and skipped over to us. She stopped in front of me and smiled up at me. "Hi!" she said.

"Pumpkin, this is my grandson, Russ."

I stuck my hand out to shake hers and introduced myself, "Very nice to meet you, Millie."

Instead of shaking my hand, she curtsied, so I gave her a very polite bow. Then I made the *pop* noise for her a couple times. She giggled and glanced back at Ida every so often.

"I have a little sister about your age," I told her.

"Can I see her?" Millie exclaimed with a big smile.

I kneeled down in front of her and smiled, "I'm just visiting Mitchell, and she's not here with me. But I'll tell her all about you next time I see her, Millie."

"Yay!" she yelled.

113

I popped for her again and then stood up. She gave me a big hug as I did.

"Millie, would you be a sweet pea and run to Auntie Vinney's, find her, and tell her Russ is here." Ida was direct and used her fingers to count the instructions off one, two, three.

"Yes, ma'am," Millie said, jumping up and down.

"What's his name again?" Ida asked Millie.

"Russ," Millie said.

"Good girl. Now please don't stop along the way and wander off like the last time. You hear, Pumpkin?" Ida added.

Millie looked down with a sheepish grin, "Yes ma'am."

"Alright, then. Run along," Ida said.

Millie dashed off and had already made it around the corner of the house before I could even think to say goodbye.

"Can she make it all the way to Birdy's?" I asked.

"Of course, she can! It's not even a half mile from here," Ida replied as she pointed in the direction that Millie had gone. "She's smart as a whip but kind of naughty. I have to keep my eye on that one."

"Is she your daughter?" I asked.

"Oh, heavens no," Ida snickered. "But you're such a sweet young man for asking," she said as she caressed my cheek.

"I guess I could've just walked to Birdy's if she could," I offered.

"Oh no. I'm going to keep you here so we can catch up," Ida said as she gave me another hug. "But it's getting too hot to be standing out here in the afternoon sun. Let's sit on the porch in the shade."

I'd been wondering what time it was, and each time, I remembered the Giant and my pocket watch exploding. What a day it had been! It seemed like years had gone by since Pop and I had boarded the train back in Seymour.

"Where's your hat?" Ida asked as she stepped up the two stairs to the porch.

"I lost it," I admitted with a frown as I followed her.

She ran her hands through my hair and sighed, "Well that's bad news for you, mister. You've got a family of ticks taking up residence in that shaggy mane of yours."

I hated ticks. I groaned because I knew what was coming next.

"Off with your clothes then, buster," she said with her hands on her hips.

115

I glanced up at her, hoping she was just kidding, but when she didn't laugh, I knew she wasn't.

"You heard me," she said softly. "I was there when you came into this world, Russell, so I've seen you naked before. And I reckon that I've picked more ticks off more boys than just about any other woman in Two Counties. Pop and your Uncle Walt used to bring 'em home by the dozens. And I've picked ticks off Birdy and Ray a million times too. Prob'ly be doin' it for Frankie in a year or two." She stared down at me with her hands on her hips.

At the mention of Ray's name, I remembered our fight and hoped she wouldn't find out about it. I tried to think of an excuse to avoid stripping, but I couldn't come up with one.

As I undressed, Ida collected my clothes. "Your clothes are all wet," she remarked. She took everything and hung it on her clothesline. "They'll be dry in no time in this heat," Ida said, staring up at the sun.

We sat on the porch for quite a while as she picked ticks and other critters off my skin. She used her fingernails to pluck their heads off after she removed them from me. She could do it with one hand too! Before she killed them, she would say, "Off with his head!" in a funny voice. I tried to imitate it, but it sounded terrible. It made her giggle each time, though.

"It's a good thing for you I don't have any patients showing up soon. You'd be a sight to see," she giggled.

I moaned at the thought of introducing myself to strangers while standing there naked. *Why hello there ma'am, nice to meet you. Nice youngins you got there. Why, yes ma'am, I am naked as a jaybird.* I put it out of my head and quickly changed the subject.

"What kind of patients? Are you a doctor?" I asked.

"I am . . . a special kind of doctor who treats women and babies," she answered as she snagged another bug from my hair. "I have a small practice here and a bigger one up in Minnesota. Well, I guess the one here's not too small, though, since everyone in Two Counties comes to visit me when I'm in town."

"I don't like my doctor," I said.

She looked at me and smiled. "Sometimes I also treat clumsy boys with names like Ray, Birdy, and Frankie."

"Will you be my doctor?" I asked. And then, before I could stop myself, I said, "I didn't know women could be doctors."

"Well, if you think about it, women make the best doctors for other women . . . and for babies too." Then she thought for a moment, "Did you know most male doctors believe newborns can't feel pain. Sounds suspiciously stupid if you ask me. Don't you think?"

I nodded. It did sound stupid.

"Everyone feels pain, Russ, even newborns. Sometimes pain comes in many forms," Ida said. She stared up toward the sky again for a few moments. She seemed to be thinking.

"Will you be my doctor?" I asked again.

Ida smiled and looked into my eyes, "I will *always* take care of you, Russ. You never have to worry about that." She bent down and kissed me on the cheek. Then she took a step back, gave me a knowing look, and said, "Russ, dear, your breath smells like you've been drinking at a speakeasy full of railmen."

My eyes bugged out because I knew she'd caught me. I hoped she wouldn't tell Pop. "Yes ma'am," I said, looking down at the ground with shame. I'd never be allowed to hang out with Ray and the older boys again.

"Ray must've found you fellas some liquor, huh?" she said.

I nodded, still unable to look her in the eyes.

And then she chortled, "It was probably some of my whiskey!"

My eyes got big when she said that. I didn't know what to say. I was worried that I'd gotten everyone in trouble. But Ida laughed and put her hands on my cheeks. "Your secrets are always safe with me, my sweet boy."

I smiled and thought, *I sure like having a grandma—especially Ida!*

When she pronounced me bug free, we went inside the house to a small room with a sink right off the front porch. It felt weird to still be naked.

Ida motioned for me to stand in front of the sink while she found a rag and some soap. Then she scrubbed me clean. I wanted to tell her that I already knew how to wash myself, but she didn't seem interested at that particular moment, and I didn't want to upset her.

Ida wasn't gentle like Mom was, though. She scrubbed me like I was covered in axle grease, and I wondered if I'd have any skin left when she was finished. But I didn't fidget or complain because I didn't want her to think I was a baby.

When she finally stopped, she looked me over and said with a satisfied smile, "That'll do." Then she went to a small chest and removed a blanket, handed it to me, and said, "Now cover yourself, Russ, or you'll scare every Baptist in Two Counties walking around like that."

The blanket was big and soft. I wrapped it around me then walked around the farmhouse for a bit. It was different from any house I'd ever seen. The furniture appeared modern and clean, and the kitchen seemed newer than ours back in Seymour.

"You thirsty?" Ida asked.

"Yes, ma'am," I said politely. "But no more Rebel Joe for me, thank you."

Ida laughed so hard that she had to blow her nose and wipe away tears with her hankie. When she finally settled down, she said seriously, "You didn't drink out of any cricks, did you? I don't want you coming down with the typhoid fever."

"No, ma'am," I fibbed. I had drunk from the brook in the cave with Birdy and the guys. But Birdy said the water was safe to drink, so I figured it best to keep that to myself.

"Well then, go to the kitchen and get yourself a nice long drink of water," she instructed. "I swiped a bunch of the pastries from the Monon on our way down, they're in the kitchen."

"Thank you, ma'am," I said.

"You're quite welcome, kind sir," Ida responded. Then she giggled and walked out of sight.

I found the railroad pastries and began to gobble them. They tasted different from the treats on the B & O. But they were still delicious to me. I hadn't realized how hungry I was. There were all kinds: some were cinnamon and some were chocolate. I stuffed them in my mouth until I had eaten every single one of them, except for the one with nuts all over it. Then I drank directly from Ida's sink in the kitchen. I didn't think to ask for a cup until after I'd finished and wiped my mouth on the blanket.

I walked outside and inspected Ida's garden again. It was one of the prettiest gardens I'd ever seen. Unlike the gardens back home, which had regular plants like corn, peas, and potatoes, Ida's garden had all sorts of colorful flowers and oddly shaped plants that I'd never seen before.

The air had grown hotter as the day progressed, and the gentle wind felt warm on my face. I was so tired that I shuffled over to the porch and lay down on Ida's swing. I yawned and rocked back and forth in the breeze. I stretched out my body and tried to relax, but I couldn't shut off my thoughts of Rebel Joe and Ray and the Giant. I hoped the rest of the day would be uneventful.

Ida came out of the house and sat next to me on the swing, gently placing my head in her lap. As I gazed up at her, I noticed she had freckles—light ones that I could only see from close up. She smiled and stroked my hair. I smiled back at her.

"Tell me about your day, Russ," she said softly.

As I thought about everything that had happened, I almost started crying again. But I knew I shouldn't tell her anything. Birdy, Ray, and the other guys would get mad if I did.

"You can tell me anything, Russ, and I'll always keep it a secret," she assured me.

Even though I'd only just met her, Ida made me feel safe, and I wanted to tell her everything. I remembered telling Birdy that I wouldn't tell Pop anything, but I never said I wouldn't tell Ida, so I did. I told her about Rebel Joe and how we'd climbed the hill together. She just nodded and rubbed my hair. I figured she didn't believe me. Honestly, I wasn't sure if I believed it myself.

I also told her about the cave and that Ray and I had gotten into a fight. I even told her that I had lied to him about Pop. I was afraid she would be angry at me because she took care of Ray, but she didn't get mad at all. She just smiled, caressed my hair, and giggled a bit. "I remember your father and Walt getting into a lot of scraps when they were boys. They even came to blows now and then. I just prayed they wouldn't hurt each other too badly," she said. "You say Ray punched you in the belly?"

I nodded and pointed to my stomach. I felt like a rat for outing Ray.

"Back in Minnesota, I saw Ray lick a boy twice his size—a mean boy too—and it wasn't even a close fight. Ray beat him down hard. I don't think the other boy even got in a single punch. Ray didn't know I was watching, and I never told him I saw him fighting. I guess what I'm trying to say is that if Ray only hit you once, it was probably just a warning, dear."

It sure hadn't *felt* like a warning. But I did believe her about the fight with the other boy because she was right: Ray could've pounded me into the ground if he wanted to, and I couldn't have done a thing to stop him. But he hadn't. He'd just walked away.

"I hope he doesn't hate me," I said morosely.

"You and Ray are brothers, and brothers fight from time to time," Ida stated. "I know Ray very well,

Russ, and I believe that deep down, he couldn't possibly stay mad at you for more than an hour or two. I bet the next time you see him, it will all be forgotten. And I promise you that he doesn't hate you."

"I hope so," I said weakly.

"I promise you," Ida said. Then she looked at me earnestly and continued, "But I would advise against telling him Pop hates him ever again."

I nodded my head. We sat there in silence for a few minutes as I processed everything that had happened to me that day. After a while, I decided to tell Ida about the train ride to Mitchell, walking on the roof of the passenger car, and my encounter with the Giant. After I'd told her everything I could remember, I noticed that she had tears in her eyes, and I felt horrible about it. I didn't ever want to make Ida cry, and I hoped that I hadn't scared her. I realized I should've never told her about the train. I tried as hard as I could to think of something to cheer her up. But before I could think of something, Ida spoke first. "Russ, can you make me a promise and keep it?" she asked.

I nodded.

"A man who would do something like that to a boy is a terrible, evil man. You must steer clear of men like that. So promise me, Russ, if you ever see him again, you'll run as fast as you can and find Pop. Don't let that man grab you again. Ever. You stay out of his reach. You hear?"

I hoped that I'd never see the Giant again, so I wouldn't have to run from him. Ida had put the fear of God in me, but what she said made sense. "Yes ma'am," I said sincerely. "I promise."

Ida looked at me and smiled, still running her fingers through my hair. As the swing gently swayed back and forth, she started humming a tune. It sounded sad, yet eerily familiar. As I grew tired and closed my eyes, the last thing I heard was Ida whispering, "I love my boys."

Ida, 1901

CHAPTER 10

I woke up to Pop's smiling face. I had a blinding headache, and I was confused. I reached up, grabbed for Pop, and gave him a long hug. I had no idea what time it was, where I was, or even what day it was, for that matter. My head was in a fog, and it felt like a rail spike was stuck in it. I put my arm over my eyes, but it didn't help.

I looked around and remembered I was at Ida's. I was still on the swing where I'd fallen asleep, but I didn't see Ida anywhere.

"Well, I see you met your grandmother, Russell." When Pop called me Russell, I knew it was bad. "How on earth did you get here, young man?"

I thought for a moment and remembered my promise to Birdy. I wasn't sure how to explain my encounter with Rebel Joe, so I closed my eyes and came up with a story. "I ditched the guys because I didn't want to go to the pond." I yawned. "I saw the big hill and remembered it was near town, so I climbed over it. It was easy."

"Oh, did ya now?" That was Pop's nice way of saying he didn't believe me. I hoped he wouldn't ask me any more questions.

I smiled and laughed, then Pop did too. He pretended to wrestle me a bit then picked me up and said, "You're quite a resourceful young man!"

I breathed a sigh of relief. At least for now, Pop didn't know about the cave, what happened with Ray, and my adventure with Rebel Joe. And I hoped that Ida would keep her promise and wouldn't tell Pop that I'd been drinking alcohol.

Pop put me down and pointed to the clothesline. "Go get dressed, son." I had forgotten that I was naked under the blanket. Pop turned around and walked back inside Ida's house.

My clothes were dry when I pulled them down from the line. They were nice and warm when I put them on, which felt good. I looked up at the sky and figured it must be late afternoon by then.

As I was finishing getting dressed, I heard the porch door squeak open and slam shut. Ida came out of the house, walked over to me, and smiled as she whispered, "I bet you've got a doozy of a headache."

"I do," I admitted softly.

"I bet you do," she said with a giggle. She held a dark bottle of something and a large spoon. "Take some of this, and you'll feel better in no time." She poured a large spoonful and put it into my mouth.

Whatever it was, it looked and tasted awful—even worse than the Rebel Joe! Ida gave me three doses, and I made a yucky face after each of them, but I finished it.

"What *is* that?" I asked.

"It's a secret medicine. It comes from South America," she whispered. Ida stood up and looked at me. "I hope we see each other again before you leave. And tell Pop that whenever we're both in town, you can always come here. You know, I pay Ray and Birdy money to run errands for me. Would you like to run errands for me, too, sometimes?"

"Sure!"

"Good. I'm happy to hear that," she said as she pulled me in close and gave me a squeeze. "Today has been a very special day for me because of you."

Pop came out and waved his thumb over his shoulder, motioning toward the front of the house. He seemed antsy and ready to leave, so I said goodbye to Ida. When she gave me a bunch of kisses all over my face, I didn't even wipe them off. That made Pop smile.

After Pop and I got into Uncle Walt's car, we both waved to Ida then sped away. Pop drove like a crazy man to Uncle Walt's house. It wasn't that far, so it didn't take long, but I figured it would've taken longer with a sane man driving. I counted one horse and three pedestrians that Pop almost hit on the way. Pop loved to drive fast. But the scarier his driving, the harder he laughed.

When we got back to Uncle Walt's house, Uncle Walt was hot and told Pop that Birdy had been drinking again. That made my ears perk up, and I got scared. With his hands on his hips, Uncle Walt looked at me sternly and asked if I'd been drinking too. "No, sir," I lied, but Uncle Walt didn't seem convinced. He smelled my breath and just looked at me skeptically. He must not have smelled anything suspicious, though, because he let me off the hook. Uncle Walt could be scary when he was mad. He was legendary with the belt, Birdy told me once. There wasn't a cousin in Two Counties who was safe from a skinnin' if he got Uncle Walt riled up.

I went upstairs and found Birdy asleep in bed. I was happy to be spending the night at his house. But Birdy was dead to the world, so he wasn't likely to be any fun. And after a while, I was bored stiff sitting in Birdy's room listening to him snore like a freight train. They shouldn't have let Birdy drink.

I decided to lay down in Birdy's room a bit. By that time, I wasn't tired anymore, and my headache had disappeared. Ida was a darn good doctor as far as I was concerned. I felt like a million bucks as I lay on the makeshift bed set up in Birdy's room. I looked up at the ceiling and decided to nickname the bed "the Rack" because it was almost as comfortable as one. As I lay there, I thought about my day again: Pop, the Giant, Ray, Rebel Joe, and, of course, Ida. I had to find a way to get out of Birdy's room somehow. I was getting restless.

I heard Pop and Uncle Walt coming up the stairs. I rolled over and pretended to be asleep. One of them opened the door and paused. I didn't move, I just breathed slowly. Birdy was still sawing logs, his bed rattling with each breath.

I heard the door close as Uncle Walt whispered, "They'll probably be asleep 'til tomorrow. Can you imagine being a kid in this day and age?" They both laughed, but I couldn't make out anything else they said as they walked down the stairs. I got up and put my ear to the door. I thought I heard something about a meeting, but I couldn't be sure. After I heard the front door open and close, the house was silent.

I opened Birdy's door slowly and tiptoed down the stairs and into the front room. As far as I could tell, no one was in the house except Birdy and me, which was strange because the place had been full of people when Pop and I had arrived. It even appeared that Aunt Vinney and Frankie were gone. I peeked out the window but didn't see anyone out front. However, I could hear Uncle Walt and Pop talking out back.

I didn't want Pop or Uncle Walt to see me, so I crept quietly toward the back of the house. As I glanced above the fireplace, I noticed Uncle Walt's rifle. It looked exactly like Rebel Joe's! I tried to recall what kind of rifle Rebel Joe said he had, but I couldn't remember.

I kept crawling until I got to the kitchen in the back of the house. Aunt Vinney's kitchen wasn't nearly as nice as Ida's. I peered out a small window and saw Pop and Uncle Walt standing in front of Uncle Walt's Model T. I stayed completely still as I listened to their conversation.

"I'll buy you a drink," Uncle Walt offered.

"I need one," Pop said. "You're a good man,

Walt. I'm going to stop listening to all the bad things your wife always says about you."

They both laughed, and I almost did too, but I covered my mouth with both hands to stifle it. Pop was a funny guy. Uncle Walt cranked the engine to life on the first try. Then he and Pop hopped into the car and sped down the alley.

Realizing I was alone except for Birdy snoring upstairs, I went back to his room. I thought about waking Birdy up. Hanging around town with him would be a hoot. Plus, he'd probably be mad at me if I went without him.

"Birdy," I said.

No response. He just kept snoozing away.

"Birdy, c'mon. Let's go out for a bit," I said loud enough for everyone in Two Counties to hear me—everyone except Birdy, that is.

"Birdy likes girls and kisses them!" I teased and gave him a nudge. He just moaned, rolled over, and continued his deep slumber.

I took off my running around clothes and began putting my fancy traveling clothes on when a coin fell out of a pocket in the old overalls of Birdy's I'd been wearing.

It made a loud noise as it bounced on the ground. After I scooped it up, I held it out in front of me. *It's a quarter!* It shined bright in the sunlight coming through

Birdy's window.

I could go to Thompson's and get me a sodee pop for sure. An orange one at that. Birdy's going to miss out on a sodee pop. I looked back at him. *What a jack!* I thought.

I finished getting dressed and headed downstairs. Then I opened the back door, headed for the alley, and made my way into town.

Birdy's house was six blocks from downtown Mitchell, so it was an easy walk. After Uncle Walt started working for the railroad like Pop, they moved into town. *Birdy's family has lived both in town and out in the country,* I realized.

I'd been to Mitchell enough times to know where everything was, but it was crowded this afternoon and hard to see. I strolled up and down some of the streets. I went into each of the hotels and sat in the lobbies for a bit, but that was boring. I also walked past the opera house, but I didn't go in.

I finally made my way to Thompson's. I was thirsty again and really wanted that sodee pop. I rubbed both sides of the quarter in my pocket as I walked. I had no idea where it had come from. But good fortune had smiled upon me as Mom would say. I wondered if Ida had given it to me while I was sleeping. Or it could've been Pop, but he usually made me do something to earn money. I eagerly waited for a car and two horses to pass before I crossed the street. I was halfway across the street when I froze. Ray was standing in front of Thompson's.

He was looking right at me from the sidewalk. He stared at me for a bit then turned away. When he returned his gaze to me, he made a face. I couldn't move. I didn't say a word. Finally, he rolled his eyes and ran toward me. I closed my eyes, wondering if he was going to punch me again. I tightened my stomach muscles, bracing myself for the blow to come. Instead, he picked me up, tossed me over his shoulder, and scurried back to the sidewalk.

AOOGA! a car horn blasted. I open my eyes just in time to see the car plow over the exact spot where I'd been standing seconds before. The driver yelled some cusswords out the window as Ray carried me to the sidewalk and set me down. Ray had saved my life again—that was twice in one day! I didn't know what to say, so I blurted out, "Sorry I said Pop hates you! I lied . . . he never even told me about you 'til this morning."

Ray looked at me briefly, then he grinned. "It's OK, kid. Maybe I shouldn't have sucker punched you."

"Birdy said I deserved it 'cause I started it."

Ray chuckled, "Just because you can *hit* someone doesn't mean you should." He paused for a moment before continuing, "Anyway, you wouldn't have liked the pond much. Birdy threw up in the water five minutes after we got there and scared the Burton girls away."

I laughed so hard that snot came out of my nose. "He's snoring away at the house. I left him there a while ago," I laughed.

Ray just shook his head. I was so glad Ray liked me again. Ida told me he would. I wondered what it would be like to live with Ida and Ray. I'd miss Pop and Mom and Betty, though.

I considered telling Ray about seeing Rebel Joe, but then I thought better of it. Ray had gotten mad at Josie for believing in ghosts, and I never wanted Ray to be mad at me again, so I kept it a secret.

"What are you doing here?" I asked.

"Watching the furniture store," he said matter-of-factly as he nodded toward the brick building across the street.

I pulled the quarter out of my pocket. It gleamed in the sunlight as I showed it to Ray and said, "You wanna get a sodee pop?" I hoped he would. *Shoot,* I thought, *I'll buy him three sodee pops if he wants, just so I can spend more time with him.*

Ray reached into his pocket and pulled out two quarters. They sparkled in the sunlight too. "Got one from Pop for watching you and one from Ida for watching the furniture store," he said. "Guess I didn't quite earn the one from Pop, though."

"I'll buy you one!" I exclaimed. I felt real grown-up to offer.

"Maybe in a bit," Ray said as he lightly pushed me behind him. I examined him while he continued to watch the store across the street. He pulled out his watch, looked at it, and furrowed his brow. And then I saw the pocket watch. It looked exactly like mine—like the one I *used* to have before the Giant caused me to lose it. Whenever I asked Pop what time it was, we'd pull out our identical watches at the same time and crack up. I dreaded having to tell Pop that I lost it and how. I figured he'd be disappointed in me.

"Do you want to see it?" Ray asked, snapping me out of the trance I'd been in.

"Sure!" I said.

Ray tossed it to me quick, which scared me because I worried that I'd drop it. But I didn't. I looked up at him with an alarmed look, but he just smiled at me then went back to staring across the street. I gave the pocket watch a good once over. It was identical to mine in every way except for a couple scratches I'd added to mine since I got it. I rubbed it with both my hands like I used to rub mine to warm it up. It shined even brighter than the quarters Ray and I had.

"What's wrong?" Ray asked.

"Pop gave me one just like this for Christmas, but when the rail marshal pushed me through the window this morning, it fell out of my pocket and smashed into a million pieces on the tracks." I got angry just thinking about it. I hated the Giant like I'd never hated anyone ever before.

Ray nodded but didn't say anything. He patted his pants and then he yelled, "Dammit!"

"What's wrong?" I asked.

"I'm out of smokes," he said. Then Ray looked inside Thompson's Drugstore and nudged me away from the door. Then he walked around the corner and motioned for me to follow him into the alley. He looked at me with a serious look on his face and said, "Gimme your quarter."

CHAPTER 11

Reluctantly, I handed Ray my quarter, while secretly hoping he'd give it back. Ray closed his hand around all three quarters and looked me in the eye. "OK, between us, we got seventy-five cents, which means I can buy seven packs of Lucky Strikes. Old Man Thompson's Seven for Seventy-Five sale is still on, and I'm out of smokes. Can you help me out?"

"Sure . . . ," I said suspiciously, "but I wanted to get a sodee pop and your smokes will use up all the money." I immediately regretted saying that and hoped Ray wouldn't get mad at me again.

But instead, Ray knelt down in front of me and talked slow and steady, like Pop would, "Tell you what, Russ . . . you let me keep this here quarter, and I'll let you keep the watch."

At first, I thought he was pulling my leg. But he didn't smile or say, "fooled you," or anything like that. He just stared at me with his dark eyes then said, "I don't want it anymore, anyway."

"Yes!" I shouted.

Ray waved his hands, letting me know to be quiet, but I was so happy to get my watch back. I still wanted a sodee pop, for sure, but I'd take the watch over a sodee pop any day! Ray gave me a firm handshake and looked me in the eye. Then he handed me the three quarters and took back the watch. I didn't understand why until he explained, "OK, here's the plan. Old Man Thompson won't sell me cigarettes anymore. But he'll sell them to you as long as you say they're for Pop. Pop smokes Lucky Strikes, that's his brand. Old Man Thompson won't think a runt like you would be smoking yet."

"No way, Ray!" I protested.

"Both Pop and Ida told Old Man Thompson not to sell any to me," he said shaking his head. "Can you believe that?"

"But Pop smokes," I said.

"So does Ida!" Ray added, pointing out the hypocrisy.

"That's not fair!" I said.

"I know!" Ray said as he agreed with me. Then he smiled and knelt down in front of me again, looking me square in the eyes. I felt the muddles coming on. "Don't be afraid, kid. If this works, you get a new watch." Then he smiled wider and said, "And if it doesn't, it'll be alright. The worst that could happen is that Old Man Thompson won't sell you the smokes. If that happens, we'll still have seventy-five cents, so we'll just get sodas instead. The only jack in this is Old Man Thompson because he won't know they're for me." Then Ray jabbed his finger into my chest and taunted, "But you'll be the king of the jacks if you don't do it."

I stood still and almost got muddled. Ray's plan sounded like it might work, but I was still scared. Then again, Ray was smart, and I wanted his pocket watch more than anything in the world. Plus, I didn't want to be a jack, so I nodded my head.

Ray smiled and patted me on the shoulder. "Attaboy! OK. Now, make sure to ask Old Man Thompson to put 'em in a bag. That'll make it sound like they're really for Pop." Ray glanced over my shoulder then looked back at me and said, "Alright, now go on in. I'll wait here."

Ray pushed me toward the front of the drugstore. I took a few steps forward then turned to look back at him. He nodded and gave me a thumbs-up. I rounded the corner and went into the store. I still didn't want to do it, but for Ray, I would give it a try.

Thompson's was bigger than any drugstore back home. It had a larger soda fountain and a lot more aisles. The place was huge and the fans on the ceiling were spinning rapidly! I wondered if Ray would beat me up if I got a sodee pop instead of the smokes. Yep, I figured I'd get a good pounding, for sure—and probably rightly so.

There were two people waiting in line: a man and a woman. I stood behind them both. The man nodded to Old Man Thompson and left. Then the lady stepped up to the counter, pointed at the wall, and asked Mrs. Thompson for something. By then, two more men had gotten in line behind me. The lady in front of me paid, then turned around and smiled at me before heading toward the door. I closed my eyes, took a deep breath, and exhaled slowly.

"What can I get for you, son?" Old Man Thompson asked.

"Seven packs of Lucky Strikes, sir," I replied.

Old Man Thompson burst into laughter while his wife gave me a startled look. Then the two men behind me started to chuckle too. *I knew this wouldn't work!* I thought as my cheeks reddened. But I didn't say anything, and I didn't move. I didn't want to disappoint Ray, so I just kept smiling at Old Man Thompson.

"Aren't you a little young to be smoking, sonny?" Mr. Thompson asked. Although I heard more guffaws from behind me, I just smiled and tried to remain calm.

"Oh, I don't smoke, sir. I'm too young, and I can't stand the smell." That much was true. "These are for Pop. He told me to get 'em for him and said to ask you to put 'em in a bag for him." My hands were sweaty, and my mouth was parched.

Mrs. Thompson's eyes widened as she smiled and examined me. "Oh, Tom! It's Pop's little boy!" she exclaimed. "He looks just like a young Pop!"

Then an idea came to me. "Howdy, ma'am! I'm Pop Jr.," I said with a huge grin for Mrs. Thompson. I appreciated the nickname Rebel Joe had given me. I owed him one.

Old Man Thompson didn't seem convinced. He studied me, but I didn't react, and I didn't stop smiling. "Well, you couldn't be anyone else but Pop's son, that's for sure," he said. But then he furrowed his brow and cocked his head to the side slightly as he grumbled, "Did Ray put you up to this?"

It was really hard to lie when he said that, but I kept my composure. I didn't know what else to say, except, "Who's Ray?"

Old Man Thompson just stared at me. Mrs. Thomson had a shocked look on her face, but she kept smiling at me as she whispered something into Mr. Thompson's ear. I didn't catch it all, but I heard enough to know she told him that I probably didn't know Ray. When Old Man Thompson looked back at me, his face was flush. I kept going just for good measure.

"Who is Ray, sir?" I asked again, sounding perplexed.

Mr. Thompson coughed and then stammered, "Sorry son.... I ... uh ... I must've gotten you confused with someone else." He smiled weakly, grabbed seven packs of Lucky Strikes from behind the counter, and opened a bag with a snap of the wrist. Then he dropped them in and handed me the bag. "Can I get you anything else, Pop Jr.? How 'bout a soda?"

I groaned inside. I wanted a sodee pop more than anything else in the world except for the watch, but I didn't have any money left because of my deal with Ray.

"No, thank you, sir." I handed him the three quarters and turned to walk out the door.

"Give our regards to Pop!" Mrs. Thompson hollered.

"Yes ma'am," I replied as I exited the door. When I turned the corner into the alley, Ray noticed the bag and smiled. He snatched it out of my hand and looked inside. Then he ruffled my hair and said with a grin, "Way to go!"

He motioned for me to follow him, so I did. We walked around the back of Thompson's and then doubled back up to Main Street. Ray looked across the street at the furniture store for a bit before saying to me, "Well done, kid. You're alright." Ray continued to watch the furniture store, but then he glanced at me and said with a laugh, "I'm gonna have to stop listening to all the bad things Birdy says about you."

I chuckled and asked, "So the watch is mine now?"

"Yep, all yours."

After Ray handed me the watch, I rubbed it again with both hands like I used to do with my old one. I was thirsty but happy.

Ray opened one of the packs of Lucky's, took out a cigarette and pulled some matches out of his pocket. He lit his smoke and breathed out smooth. He looked down at me watching him. "You want one?" he offered.

"Yeah!" I exclaimed.

He chuckled and gave me one. I put it in my mouth like I'd seen Pop do a million times. Ray lit the end and then said, "Just breathe in like you're drinking through a straw."

I did exactly what he said, but I instantly regretted it. My lungs convulsed as I coughed out the smoke along with a large wad of spit. Even when the smoke was out of my lungs, I couldn't stop coughing. Ray watched me with a smile on his face, then turned his attention back to the furniture store.

After getting my breath back, I watched how he took a deep drag of the cigarette then exhaled easily. I didn't want to smoke anymore, but I took another drag just to try again. This time, it was even worse! I convulsed and coughed so much I dropped to my knees.

Ray looked down at me unconcerned, "Keep practicing," he said with a wink.

"OK . . ." I managed to croak out. I took another drag and hacked even worse than before. I hated smoking.

Ray stood with his back against the wall of the building we were standing next to and continued to smoke like a seasoned pro.

"Are we going back to Rebel Joe's cave tonight," I asked between coughs.

Ray shrugged. He took a couple steps toward the street and stared at the furniture store intently.

"Why do you keep looking at the furniture store?" I asked.

"Ida wanted me to watch out for Uncle Walt," Ray answered.

"He's with Pop," I said.

"Nope. . . . Pop left ten minutes after they got there."

Wow! Ray was good at spying!

"Ida said she'd pay me to run errands for her next time we're all in town," I boasted. "Maybe she'll ask me to spy on someone too?"

"Good for you, kid," Ray sneered. He seemed unimpressed. "Ida pays well."

"Ida's great!" I beamed.

Suddenly Ray got really serious. He looked at me then back at the furniture store and said, "Stay here."

I watched as Ray walked across the street to the furniture store. He poked his head inside the door and then went inside. I wondered why he was spying on Uncle Walt and why Ida would pay him to do so. Either way, it was all extremely exciting.

While Ray was out of sight, I walked over to the side of the alley and stubbed out my cigarette. I didn't want Ray to think I wasn't grateful for him bumming me a smoke, but I didn't want the rest of it. In fact, I was starting to feel sick to my stomach. I leaned back up against the wall and put my hand over my eyes to try to feel better. A few minutes went by as I waited for Ray to come back. I hoped he hadn't ditched me.

I was starting to feel a bit better and was considering going to look for Ray when I saw him leave the furniture store. I breathed a sigh of relief. Ray motioned for me to meet him across the street, so I waited for a horse to go by. Then I ran across the street, narrowly avoiding a steaming pile of fresh horse manure. I caught up to Ray as he walked away from the furniture store. "Uncle Walt's passed out," he said. "You head back to the house, and don't say anything to anyone. You hear me?"

I nodded. "But why is Uncle Walt passed out in a furniture shop?" I asked.

"There's a speakeasy in back. It's secret, you know, because of Prohibition." After a brief pause, he continued, "Well, I guess it's not so secret. Every railman in Two Counties was in there just now. The judge told me he would drive Uncle Walt home in a bit. So I'm going to take Uncle Walt's car."

Wow! I thought. *This is so exciting!* "Can I go with you?" I asked.

"No. Go back to Uncle Walt's like I told you!" Ray demanded.

"OK. OK," I said. I didn't want to go back to Uncle Walt's, but I also didn't want to make Ray mad. As he began to walk away, I shouted, "Thanks for the watch!"

Ray stopped and looked at me despondently for a second then nodded his head.

I was still stunned. He had traded me his watch for a quarter! And it looked just like my old one. It was as if I'd never lost mine. *Having a brother is complicated,* I thought. *I hope Ray is the only brother that Mom and Pop haven't told me about. One is enough!*

As I made my way toward Uncle Walt's place, I kept thinking about Ray. I was happy that we were friends again, and I hoped I could hang around with him some more. I had so much fun fooling Old Man Thompson that I decided to call it the Great Cigarette Caper.

CHAPTER 12

D owntown Mitchell hadn't thinned out much while I was with Ray, so I took my time walking up the sidewalk. It was also still hotter than hades outside, and I had to stop to cough every few seconds too. I promised myself then and there that I'd never smoke again.

The streets were crowded with cars, carts, and horses, and the odor of gasoline fumes and horse poop reminded me of downtown Seymour. A cacophony of people talking and bells ringing, whistles blowing, and horns honking filled the air. Downtown Mitchell was alive and happening, and I didn't want to go back to Birdy's just to listen to him snore for the rest of the evening.

But Ray had told me to go back to Uncle Walt's, and I was really thirsty, so I figured that was probably the best idea anyway, so I could get something to drink.

Then I remembered the train depot, which had a big water fountain. I could get a nice long drink there and then stay out some more. No way was I going to let Birdy waste my only evening out on the town in Mitchell. I figured no one would miss me at Uncle Walt's as long as I got back before dark. And it wouldn't be dark at least another hour. I verified that by pulling out my new pocket watch and checking the time.

That decided, I made the trek to the train depot. I liked to watch the people at the depot back home and make up stories about them. The Mitchell depot wasn't too far out of the way, so I turned around and headed in that direction.

I quickened my pace because my throat was parched, and I really needed a long, cool drink. As I approached the depot, I heard a train whistle scream. Smoke and steam were billowing out from the train's engine as I approached from the front. The train was a 2-8-2 Mikado with 63-inch drive wheels, and it was spewing out steam like an angry wife whose husband forgot her birthday. I took a step back to study the mass of modern machinery. The cab was painted B & O Blue as was part of the boiler. And the sharp steel wheels gleamed like mirrors. I wondered for a moment where the train was headed. Wherever it was, this beauty would get the passengers where they were going.

I strolled down the platform and practiced my popping for a spell. I noticed the clock at the depot, and I checked my new pocket watch. It was spot on.

"Yes!" I said to myself.

I thought for a moment and tried to remember the timetables. *This must be the daily 86—a third-class train.* Nobody liked to ride third class, not even country folk. I ripped off a loud cow moo—loud enough that more than one adult turned and stared at me. Sure enough, the locomotive was pulling both freight and coach this evening, as third-class trains almost always did. Riding third class meant the engineer had to pull over for any first-class and second-class trains steaming the opposite direction, so it would be a long boring ride. But I remembered from the timetables that it was the last train east for the night, so I figured whoever was boarding didn't have much of a choice.

This train will be passing right by my house in a couple of hours. That made me think about home again and how much I missed Mom. For a moment, I even thought about hopping the train and just going home now. We only lived five minutes from the depot in Seymour. I had walked it a million times. But then I wondered what I would say to Mom when I got home. *Hi Mom! Sorry to wake you up, I hopped the 86 and came home. But I didn't tell Pop, and now I'm home.* That's as far as I got in my mind before Mom came at me with broom or hit me with the Ouchy Spoon from the kitchen. I laughed to myself. It would probably be faster to walk home than take the 86, so I figured I'd stay in Mitchell for the evening as planned.

I saw the water fountain shining in the sun like a watery oasis in the desert. I ran as fast as I could, narrowly missing a porter, and was standing in front of it in the blink of an eye. I bent down and felt the cool water hit my lips; it tasted so good. After a bit, a nice-looking lady got in line behind me, so I stopped drinking and made way for her. She smiled and thanked me. I moved and stood behind her since there was no one else waiting. She giggled when she walked away, saying, "Leave some for the rest of the townsfolk, darlin'."

When I finally quenched my thirst, I no longer tasted the cigarette in my mouth. But my belly practically sloshed as I walked. So I sat down on a bench and studied the train. It wasn't a long one. Pop said the late trains pulled the least number of cars. The B & O blue caboose brought up the rear. I'd loved cabooses my whole life, and this one shined like a coin in the sun. Normally, trains pulling passenger coaches didn't have cabooses, but this express was hauling freight too. Pop said trains didn't need cabooses anymore, but I hoped he was wrong.

Unlike the rest of Mitchell, the depot wasn't crowded. But making up stories about people wasn't much fun, so I got up and continued my stroll down the platform. As I walked, I noticed a man and a woman hurrying to hop on the train. The porter helped the woman up the steps. I strained my eyes to see some other men standing toward the back of the train.

Then I saw him and stopped dead in my tracks. It was Pop—he was at the depot, standing next to the caboose talking to two railmen. Pop seemed to be doing all the talking, though, while the men just nodded. The two men glanced at each other and smiled before saying something to Pop.

I was scared for a moment, but then I realized that I didn't have any reason to be scared. After all, Pop didn't know anything about Ray and the smokes. I sniffed my hands to make doubly sure I didn't smell like a cigarette. They smelled OK to me, so I decided to see what Pop was doing. I figured he might even buy me a sodee pop at the depot. Seeing Pop made me so happy I felt the evening couldn't get any better. After having a nice refreshing orange sodee pop, I figured I'd probably be tired enough to go to sleep back at Uncle Walt's house.

I noticed Pop hand each of the men something. The men exchanged a glance, then shrugged and walked away. As I made my way toward Pop, I waved to him and called his name. He looked around a bit, but I guessed he hadn't seen or heard me, so I tried again. But before I knew what was happening, Pop jumped on the train!

I ran toward him, shouting his name. *Why did Pop board the train?* I hollered for him again, but he couldn't hear me over the din of the train. I was scared that Pop was going home and leaving me in Mitchell. I couldn't think of any other reason why Pop would be getting on a train that was heading home. And then I wondered if Pop had left Ray this way.

When the whistle shrieked twice, the train began to move. I could smell the acrid smoke from the train, then my mind began playing tricks on me: it looked like the train was standing still and the platform was moving backward. I saw a man sprint from the depot and jump on one of the passenger cars. Pop always said to think things through, but this time, I just took off running for the train.

I ran as fast as I could, grabbed onto the nearest handrail, and pulled myself onto the vestibule between the first and second passenger cars. As the train began to accelerate, I gazed out from the vestibule and watched the town begin to race by. I had no idea why I'd just jumped the train. *Pop will skin me for sure when he finds out.* I thought about hopping back off the train, but, by then, it was going too fast, so I made my way into the nearest passenger compartment.

The car was almost empty. Pop had boarded the train toward the rear car, so I decided to head that way. But when I turned around, I ran right into the conductor coming through the door. "Do you have a ticket, son?" he asked. He looked like a mean old man.

"Huh?" was all I managed to say.

"Did you just jump my train, son?" he barked.

Pop had told me they could throw you off a moving train for that. My heart thumped inside my chest and my mind went blank as I tried to come up with an answer.

The conductor cleared his throat and said firmly, "Am I going to have to alert the rail marshal, son?" Then he grabbed my arm and walked me forward into the first passenger car. He pulled me up the aisle as passengers looked up and gave me strange looks. I wondered if going to jail might be better than facing Pop. *No*, I figured. *But it would be better than facing Mom, for sure.*

"We got us another jumper," the conductor said to a porter at the front of the car.

"He's not a jumper," the porter said. "That's Pop's boy. That's young Russ." I looked up to see Leonard smiling down at me.

"Yeah!" I exclaimed, yanking my arm away from the conductor. "I'm Pop Jr."

The conductor scrutinized me for a minute and didn't say anything. I wasn't happy at the prospect of getting thrown off the train or going to jail. But then the conductor's expression changed, and he said, "Well, I'll be. You look just like Pop. I saw him outside right before we left. Where is he?"

I raised a shaky finger and pointed toward the rear of the train. "He's in the back talking to someone," I said. But in reality, I had no idea where Pop was or what he was doing. I could tell this wasn't going to end well for me.

"OK, son. Sit here," the conductor said, pointing at an empty seat. "And don't get into any trouble." Then he left and began collecting tickets.

Leonard walked up and shook my hand, "Good evening, young Russ. What on earth are you and Pop doing on the 86?"

I had no idea why either of us was on the train, but I couldn't tell Leonard that. "Last train east," I quickly replied.

"That's fo' sure. But you know you can walk to Seymour faster than this here train will get you there, don't ya?" Leonard chuckled.

"I've heard that," I said nodding my head.

"I got to get to work now, but if you need anything, just holler," Leonard said. Then he patted me on the head and continued down the aisle.

I sat down and just stared straight ahead. Then I put my head in my hands. *Why did I jump the train? Pop wouldn't leave me forever. Mom would murder him. And I knew how to get home. I've really messed up this time. I should've just stayed the night with Birdy. I wish I could do this whole day over!*

I tried to come up with an excuse to give Pop so he wouldn't be mad at me—or worse, disappointed in me. Disgusted with myself, I looked out the window and thought again about the day I'd had. It had been a pretty crazy day, but I was glad I got to meet my brother Ray. And he did trade me his watch for a quarter. That was a pretty swell thing for him to do. I hoped I'd get to see Ray again soon.

After a while, the train steamed into Rivervale. As it slowed to a stop, I thought about getting out and walking back to Mitchell. But I knew it would be a long walk, and it would be dark before I got back, so I just sat in my seat as a few passengers got off.

It was stuffy in the coach. I took off my jacket and laid it on the seat. I knew the train would cross the East Fork in a short while, and I wanted to watch it from the vestibule. Leonard was at the front of the car with his back turned to me. I looked around for the conductor, but I didn't see him, so I got up and walked to the back of the passenger car. I checked on Leonard one more time then opened the door and slid through as quiet as I could.

There were two men in the vestibule puffing on cigars. As soon as I smelled the smoke, I wondered if it was Pop. But it wasn't. They both smiled and nodded to me. I responded by saying, "Gentlemen," in a distinguished voice to mimic how Pop would say it.

The next car was fairly full, and none of the passengers looked happy. But I wasn't happy, either. I got long glances and glares as I made my way rearward. By the time I made it to the back of the car, I just glared back. I was tired of being nice. I opened the door to the vestibule and left the angry car behind me. I groaned when I saw three men on the vestibule. But none of them were Pop, which I figured was good. I wasn't ready to see him and have him ask what I was doing on the train.

I gave them a friendly nod and was reaching for the door to the next car when one of them spoke up, "I don't think you're allowed to go back there, young man."

As I opened the door, I turned and quickly said, "My pop's back there."

Strangely the next passenger car was empty except for a man snoozing away about halfway back. His snoring reminded me of Birdy's. This train ride was turning out to be really strange. I didn't have much time to ponder it, though, because the far door opened and the conductor started making his way through the car. He'd told me to stay up front and not get into trouble, and I had failed at both. Fortunately, he was talking to a porter behind him, so his head was turned and he hadn't seen me. Quick as a jackrabbit, I dropped to the floor, crawled under one of the seats, and stayed quiet and completely still.

". . . I don't know why, but when I'm told what to do, I do it, and I don't make chitchat," the conductor said as he walked up the aisle while talking to the porter. "I think he's the only one in here," he said after a moment. "Sir . . ." the conductor said softly to the snoring man. Then after a few seconds of silence, the conductor tapped the man on the shoulder and said, "I'm terribly sorry, sir, but we need to do some maintenance on this car. Would you be so kind as to move to the next car forward? Again, I apologize."

I heard the man cough and then say, "Sure thing."

A few seconds later, I saw three sets of feet walk by me. I remained still and quiet so as not to get caught. Soon, I heard the door open, the sound of their footsteps shuffle on the vestibule, and then the door close. I smiled to myself thinking I had gotten away with it. I waited another minute in silence just to make sure, then I poked my head out from beneath the seat and took a cautious look around. The car was empty. I wondered what kind of maintenance they had to perform but quickly put it out of my mind.

As I continued making my way toward the rear of the train, I stopped in the vestibule. It was empty, so I let out a sigh of sincere relief. The warm breeze coming from the open window felt good on my face. The train was almost to the bridge over the East Fork, which was my favorite view in the world. I was glad that I hadn't missed it. As the train headed downhill toward the East Fork, I could see the sides of the valley as they followed the river downstream. The view was magnificent and stretched on for miles—as far as my eyes could see.

There must've been a million trees covering either side of the valley, and the river below was the prettiest one in the world. I spotted two boys fishing in a boat on the river, and we waved to each other.

As the train chugged back out of the river valley, I remained in the vestibule watching the trees zoom past. As the train rounded a bend along the river—the same river that Pop and I fished in back home—I thought about what I was going to say to him. I wanted to go find him, but I didn't know what he would say—or do. Maybe a smack in the mouth? Certainly, a stern talking to. He'd think of me as a kid again, and he'd be disappointed in me, for sure. After thinking about it for a while, I decided I'd just tell him the truth—that I'd hopped the train because I saw him and didn't want to be left behind. Either way, I was in deep trouble, so I figured, why make it worse. I decided to wait one more stop before I went to face the music.

As the train neared Tunnelton, the whistle sounded and the locomotive began to slow down. I stayed in the vestibule while the train stopped. A bunch of passengers got off and one got on.

The train began to move again—slowly at first then faster as it tried to gather speed to make it up the hill out of Tunnelton. I noticed I was still wearing my T-shirt and had left my jacket up front, so I decided to go get it before I went rearward looking for Pop. As I opened the heavy door to the passenger car, I noticed the conductor talking to someone. When the conductor turned and walked forward, the man he'd been talking to looked right at me. It was the Giant.

CHAPTER 13

The Giant grinned at me, but it wasn't a friendly smile; it was the same crazy man's smile I'd seen earlier in the day. I heard Ida's voice inside in my head say: "If you ever see him again, . . . run as fast as you can and find Pop." But I just froze. I got really muddled when the Giant turned and slowly lumbered down the aisle toward me. I knew I had to run, but I felt so weak that I couldn't move.

By then, the Giant was halfway down the aisle, still grinning and still coming for me. *Find Pop,* I thought. *Find Pop.* When the Giant reached into his jacket, I was finally able to make my feet move.

I took one step back, returned to the vestibule, and slammed the door in the Giant's face. Then I scampered into the following passenger car just as the train whistle shrieked again three times. But before I could slam that door in the Giant's face, he reached out, grabbed my hair, and pulled me back into the vestibule.

I screamed as he yanked me closer. He clutched my hair in his right hand, but I couldn't see his left hand. I assumed he was reaching for his Colt. Knowing there was no way I could break free, I figured I was going to die right there.

But instead, the Giant covered my mouth with his left hand. "Shut up!" he hissed. It was hard to breathe with his enormous paw covering my mouth. I squirmed and kicked and tried to get free, but his grip on me was too tight. I tried to think of a plan. I was so angry at myself for not being able to get away from him and because I'd let him catch me in the first place. But all day, I'd been thinking about what I'd do if he ever grabbed me again, so I had a plan. It was a big risk and could get me killed, but I figured I was a goner anyway, so I didn't think there was much else to lose.

I let my body go limp. When he started shaking me, I kept my body as limp as I could and didn't react. When he shook me again, I didn't move a muscle. I didn't even breathe. It was then that the Giant did what I'd been hoping he'd do. He removed his hand from my mouth to take a better look at me, and when he did, I leaned forward and bit down on his large left hand as hard as I could, like I was eating a tough piece of meat. I sunk my teeth so deep into his skin that I ripped off a chunk of his hand. The Giant howled like a banshee, grabbed his hand, and let me go. I slid to the floor, noticing that I'd torn through the skin and muscle all the way to the bone, which was sticking out.

I jumped up as fast as I could and opened the door to the passenger car. But before the door closed behind me, the Giant grabbed me by my T-shirt. I quickly turned around, pushed on the door as hard as I could, and slammed it on his left hand, the same one that I'd just bitten. I slammed the door on his hand again and again with all my might. The Giant wailed and fell to his knees just as the door finally closed.

I ran down the aisle as fast as I could. I quickly scanned for passengers but there weren't any. And I remembered the conductor moving everyone forward. Only Pop could help me now. When I heard the door open behind me, I didn't look back. I knew who it was. I had to find Pop before the Giant grabbed me again. I continued sprinting toward the rear of the train.

When I reached the door in the back of the passenger car, I twisted the handle, but it only moved halfway. I tried again, but it was stuck. I started to panic as the Giant slowly closed in on me.

I tried the door again. This time, I jumped up and put all my weight on the handle. Miraculously, the door opened! I fell through and landed on my stomach in the vestibule. I inhaled deeply and quickly opened the next door toward the rear of the train. As I made my way through the car, I heard the door crash closed behind me. Pop wasn't in this car, either. It was empty too.

I groaned loud then ran as fast as I could through the car. I looked forward once I opened the door to the vestibule, but I didn't see the Giant at all. As I caught my breath, I noticed that the next car was the caboose.

Relief flooded over me. *Of course, Pop would be in the caboose. I should've guessed that when I first got on.* Pop worked for the railroad, so he could go in the caboose anytime he wanted. Pop was probably on the back porch of the caboose smoking a cigar.

I turned the handle of the door to the caboose, but it was locked. I pounded on the door and waited.

And waited. And waited.

No one answered. I put my ear to the door and listened, but I didn't hear a thing coming from the caboose. I worried that I'd waited too long, and the Giant would be coming through the door at any moment.

Suddenly, I realized that if Pop wasn't in the caboose, there was no way he was on the train. Reality came crashing down on me like a ton of bricks. Pop wouldn't have left me in Mitchell without telling me he was leaving. I know I saw him hop on the train, but I never checked to see if he'd jumped back off. So Pop must've gotten off the train before it left the depot in Mitchell. Maybe he'd only boarded to say hello to one of his friends, or to grab a parcel, or any number of reasons, but then he got back off for sure. It was the only explanation that made sense because Pop wasn't on this train. I thought about Pop's mystery novels again. Sherlock Holmes would've said that if you rule out the impossible, whatever was left was the truth.

The Giant was coming to kill me. That much I knew was true. I slowly opened the door to the next car forward and saw the Giant wrapping his hand with a dark piece of cloth. "I'm gonna hurt you real bad, boy," he snarled. I'd never seen anyone so angry. As he started coming toward me, I closed the door and looked around. I was trapped. I didn't know what to do or how to get away.

Then I looked to my left and saw the open window of the vestibule. It was my only escape route. It certainly wasn't a good one, but I was running out of options. I climbed into the window and sat with my legs dangling over the edge. Then I reached over to the ladder and shimmied up, hand over hand, until I was almost to the top. It seemed a lot easier to climb than it had been that morning.

Just as I reached the top of the train, I heard the door open to the vestibule. It had to be the Giant, so I stayed silent and held my breath. I didn't think he'd heard me get on the roof. I waited for a moment and listened, but I couldn't hear anything over the sound of the steam engine and the rattle of the wheels clanking on the tracks.

I started to inch my way toward the front of the car, figuring that once I got to the next car, I could climb down and sneak back in. But I had to get there quickly because I didn't know when the Giant would wise up and realize where I was. So I got up on my hands and knees and began to make my way forward to the next car.

The roof was fairly flat. Five vents were spaced evenly across the roof of the passenger car. I reached for the first one and held on to it, but my legs swung to and fro, and for a moment, I thought I was going to slide off the top of the train. I wiggled my legs until they were back to the center of the roof, and then I braced myself because the train whistle screamed three times.

I craned my neck and looked off into the distance and saw the Big Tunnel. I could just barely make out the words *BIG TUNNEL* above it. I felt like my heart was going to leap out of my chest.

I looked behind me and wondered about going back down the way I'd come up. But the Giant would be there, and surely by now, he'd figured out where I'd escaped to. When I remembered that I'd actually bit off part of his hand, I laughed for a second then started to shake. *He'll kill me for sure if he catches me,* I thought. *Birdy will never believe this . . . assuming I live to tell him about it.*

The whistle blew another three times, which reminded me of the fast-approaching tunnel. Once again, I was trapped: there wasn't enough clearance above the train for me to make it through the tunnel, and there was a murderous giant behind me. If I stayed on the roof, I'd get squished. If I went back, the Giant would kill me. And if I jumped off the train, I would surely break every bone in my body. I didn't like my chances, but I decided to go forward.

Slowly, I stood up and began to walk forward. After a couple steps, it seemed easier than I thought it would be, so I relaxed a bit and took another step. I passed the first and then the second vent. The next vent was only two more steps away. *I'm train walking! I'm a train walker!*

As I took another step, the train lurched to the left, and I lost my footing and fell. I hit the top of the roof hard. The watch Ray had just given me fell out of my pocket and slid toward the edge of the roof.

"No!" I yelled. I tried to grab it, but it was just out of reach. But then I started sliding toward the edge of the roof.

"No!" I shouted again. The darkish-green blur of the trees rushing by made me blink my eyes and lose focus. But as I slid, I snapped up the watch and grabbed the vent with my other hand.

When the train swayed back, I slid with it, put the watch back in my pocket, grabbed the vent with both hands, and squirmed back to the center. I looked ahead and saw that the locomotive was steaming ever closer to the tunnel. I didn't have enough time to get to the front of the car, and I didn't have time to get down, either. I figured I was a dead for sure. The tunnel began to devour the train and I would be next.

My brain wouldn't allow me to run forward, but then I faintly heard a familiar voice. I couldn't make out exactly what the voice said, but I distinctly heard the word *run*. So I got up slowly, holding on to the vent. The trained jiggled back and forth, but I was able to keep my balance.

"Run forward and grab ahold of the railing! Then slide into the window!" the familiar voice hollered. "Run forward and grab ahold of the railing! Then slide into the window!" the voice repeated. It sounded like Uncle Walt!

Without even thinking, I got up and ran as fast as I could. It seemed insanely stupid to run toward the entrance of a tunnel that was swallowing the train, but that's what I did. I ran forward as fast as I could and jumped over the last two vents.

By this time, the tunnel entrance was almost on top of me. I dove to the left, grabbed the ladder next to the vestibule, and then slid down the side of the car. I tried to aim my feet so they would slide through the window, but I overshot it. I screamed as my feet hit the side of the passenger car and bounced off.

My heart was pounding as I hung off the side of the car. The tunnel was right there! I still had ahold of the ladder, though, and when my momentum swung me back toward the window, I managed to hook one leg inside. I looked ahead and saw that the tunnel entrance was so close I could practically reach out and touch it. It took all my strength, but I was finally able to thrust my other leg and then my body into the vestibule.

As soon as I fell into the vestibule, the train entered the tunnel, and everything went dark as death. I knew I was alive when my feet smacked the floor hard and my momentum threw me against the door. When I banged my head on the door handle, I dropped to the floor, and my head exploded in pain. I saw stars— honest-to-goodness stars. Until that moment, I always thought it was just a figure of speech.

I lay on the floor for some time, unable to move. In fact, I might've been unconscious for a moment. What little I could see from the dim lights of the passenger car let me know the train was still in the tunnel. For a second, I forgot what had happened, but I soon remembered. I had miraculously made it back inside the vestibule before I got crushed by the tunnel. I tried to get up, but my head was throbbing, and I heard a ringing sound in my ears. So I lay back down on the floor. I felt my arms and legs to make sure I was really there. Then I took a deep breath and started to shake.

I couldn't stop shaking. My jaw chattered like they did when I got really cold from playing in the snow. Mom called it the yakety-yaks. But I wasn't cold—I was sweating. I just lay there for a while longer, waiting for my head to stop spinning and my ears to stop ringing. I may have lost consciousness again.

When I came to, it was a bit lighter, and the sound of the train's whistle pierced my ears. I closed my eyes to shut it all out, and then I remembered that I had train walked, and I had gotten away from the Giant. But then I wondered where he was. I started to get up slowly, but I felt a little sick, so I sat back down for a moment. When I finally got to my feet, I tottered toward the front of the train. As I walked through the passenger cars, no one paid any attention to me. The train's passengers were reading newspapers, looking out the window, or sleeping. And thankfully, I didn't see the Giant anywhere.

As I opened the door of the front-most coach, I heard the familiar sound of a ukulele softly playing. I looked over and saw Leonard strumming a tune. He gave me a wink and did a couple of quick chord changes to show off.

"Pop asked if you could watch me for a bit," I fibbed, hoping he'd protect me from the Giant.

Leonard nodded his head. "Of course, I can, young Russ." He played another couple measures and winked again.

"I'm going to lie down. I'm tired," I said. Leonard nodded and continued to play.

I made my way to the front of the car and noticed the conductor was sitting down up front. He appeared to be asleep. I sat down on the seat with my jacket hanging over it. I felt safe with Leonard near me. He'd help me for sure. I exhaled a large breath. And then I started to shake again, I couldn't stop. I lay down on the seat and tried to hide myself as best I could.

After a while, I sat up. I may have been unconscious again because I didn't remember much. I had stopped shaking. By this time, it was dark out, so I guess I'd sort of lost track of time. I thought I'd heard the conductor tell Leonard that we were coming up on Sparksville, though.

My head was still foggy, and it hurt really bad. I noticed that the conductor had gotten up and was checking his roster. And I could no longer hear Leonard playing his ukulele.

I looked around but didn't see the Giant anywhere. I couldn't let myself fall asleep again. I knew I had to keep my eyes open, but it was difficult.

I wondered what I'd do when I got home. I guess I'd have to tell Mom the truth—that I took the train home by myself. She would certainly yell at me in German. Pop wouldn't be too happy with me, either. When I thought about it all, I wanted to cry, but I didn't.

Just then, I heard someone cough, and it sounded familiar. Then the coughing person walked past me. It was Pop! I couldn't believe it! He stopped at the front of the car and just stared at the wall. He hadn't seen me, so I closed my eyes and pretended to be asleep; I didn't know what else to do. I peeked with one eye and watched Pop as he continued to just stare at the front of the car like he was lost. *How did he get here?* I wondered. *How could I have missed him? I never saw him anywhere on my way back through the train.*

Then I realized there was one place I hadn't looked in any of the cars: the bathrooms. *Pop must've been in the can!* I never thought to knock on the bathroom doors. Who would? He must've been in the can a long time too. *I bet that can smells something awful! Pop can stink up a shitter worse than anyone in all of Indiana—Kentucky too!*

I pretended to look sleepy and made my voice sound like I'd just woken up. "Pop?"

Pop turned his head and looked at me. I waited for him to holler at me, but he didn't. Instead, he tried to sit down next to me, but he fell over onto the floor. He got back up quickly, dusted himself off, and looked around. I guess nobody saw him fall or nobody cared because he didn't say anything to anyone. He just sat down next to me and patted me on the back. I had no idea what to say, so I didn't say anything. After a few seconds passed, he looked over at me, blinked his eyes a couple of times, then asked, "What are you doing here?"

"I wanted to come home with you," I said. That much was true. I didn't elaborate.

Pop nodded his head and looked straight ahead. I wondered if he was drunk. Maybe he'd gotten all liquored up with Uncle Walt. If he had, maybe he'd forgotten that he and I were supposed to stay at Uncle Walt's house tonight.

No such luck. "Weren't you supposed to stay at Walt's?" he asked sternly.

I groaned inside when he looked at me like he was starting to figure things out, but I still didn't say anything. I just gave him a weak smile and shrugged. I figured I might as well see how things played out without me telling him anything, if possible. We sat there in silence for a while, and then I felt tired again, so I lay down and rested my head in Pop's lap and closed my eyes. Pop rubbed the back of my head, and I felt safe.

"You got a knot on your head, Russ," he said, rubbing his fingers over the bump on my head.

"Ouch!" I moaned. "I guess I must've hit my head when I was fooling around earlier."

Pop chuckled and said, "Well, you ought not do that. We'll have your Mom look at it when we get home."

"Yes, sir," I agreed.

I continued to rest my head in Pop's lap. I was so relieved to be with him again. I felt safe for the first time in a long time. Just then, I remembered the Giant, but he didn't scare me anymore. Pop would protect me from him. Nobody would mess with Pop. I closed my eyes and thought about Ray, again trying to grasp that I had a brother.

"Pop?" I asked.

Pop glanced down at me and said, "Yes, son."

"Can I see Ray again?"

Pop didn't say anything at first; he just stared down at me, looking sad. After a while, he said, "We'll see," as he patted my back.

"Can I spend more time at Birdy's house this summer? It's really fun there!"

Pop looked mildly annoyed as he said, "Well, Russell, you were supposed to be there right now, weren't you?"

"Yes, but when I saw you get on the train, I thought you were leaving me behind, and I got scared. But I want to go back again soon now that it's summer. Please, Pop!"

Pop looked at me and sighed, "I guess. I have to go back again tomorrow, anyway."

"Can I go with you and stay with Birdy this week? We were going to sleep outside in the tent!"

Pop looked at me hesitantly and shook his head. "I don't know, Russ."

"Please, please, *please*, Pop?"

Pop shook his head again, but this time, he

grinned as he patted me on the back. "I'll talk to Walt about it."

I smiled because whenever Pop said anything like that, it meant yes. I tried not to smile too much.

"Plus, I'm going to be working out of Mitchell for the next week."

"Thanks, Pop," I said, wrapping my arms around him in a big hug. But soon, my smile turned into a frown as I remembered the Giant again. I never wanted to ride the train again for the rest of my life. But I also didn't want to hurt Pop's feelings because I knew how much he liked to ride the rails. "Can we drive the Model T to Mitchell tomorrow instead of riding the train?" I asked quietly.

Pop looked at me suspiciously for a moment before he asked, "Why Russ?"

I thought quickly and replied, "Well, . . . you always smile when you drive, and you smile more when you drive fast." I giggled. "And I like it when you drive fast," I fibbed.

"Oh, do ya now?" Pop looked at me with one eyebrow raised and gave a deep belly laugh—a long one. He chuckled so long it made him cough. Then he said, "You know, son, that might be the best idea I've heard all day." Pop smiled and seemed to lose himself in thought. He stared ahead, and after a while, he started moving his mouth like he was thinking.

I felt happy knowing that I'd get to see both

Ray and Birdy again the next day—and Ida too. And I was still ten in Two Counties! *I might get me a sip of the Rebel Joe,* I smiled at the thought. As I closed my heavy eyelids, a wave of exhaustion rushed over me. I couldn't wait to get home to my own bed, far away from the Giant and the train.

Before I drifted off to sleep, I thought one more time of Rebel Joe—the man, not the hooch. I whispered to Pop, "I saw Rebel Joe today."

Pop chuckled and said, "I think he's dead, son."

Rebel Joe might be dead, but I remembered the voice that had told me to run when I was up on the train. That voice—the voice that had saved my life—had sounded familiar. But it wasn't the voice of Uncle Walt. It was Rebel Joe's voice.

Russ, 1934

Now that you've finished the book, I would love it if you could take a moment to share your thoughts by leaving a review. Your review will help us continue to publish more books in the Rebel Joe series.

Acknowledgments

All my stories are about family. I don't know how to tell a story without some fairly flawed family getting into trouble. So, I'd like to thank my family first. To Becky for limitless love and support. To Mom, Dad, Uncle Sandy and Nanny for all the yarns they told me over the years. To my siblings and for our shared past and adventures which will provide me with a plethora of material perpetually. And to my children, who taught me by their own excellence in music and art, that with hard work and imagination you can create happy theater. Thank you all.

To my editor, Jennifer Huston, who worked with me to lift and transform these stories from their oral roots to their final polished written prose. Her attention to detail and quality of craft in both the developmental and editing phases was both a rewarding and learning experience for me. And to Steve Grundt for the thoroughness of review and for his thoughtful advice. Thank you both.

To Yekaterina "Kat" Komarovskaya for her wonderful illustrations and art. Her ability to transform the feel of Screams of Late Spring into the look of Screams of Late Spring was wonderful to watch. And for her advice and input on the characters and the story. And to Mike Ficarra for his formatting and typography skills. Our number one goal was to present the reader with professional product in their favorite format. He did that and more. Thank you both.

To Becky Parker Geist and the whole team at Pro Audio Voices for their recording of the audiobook. It was an enjoyable and educational experience to be part of a professional production. And to Craig A. Hart for his amazing articulation as the voice of all the characters of Screams of Late Spring. In particular, Craig's portrayal of Russ, the narrator, made the story speak in a whole new way to me. Thank you all.

During my travels through Two Counties and along the railroads, I was fortunate to meet and trade stories with some amazing people. Three of them were particularly helpful on the journey that led to the publishing these twisted tall tales. Joyce Shepherd, Library Director, Lawrence County Museum of History & Edward L. Hutton Research Library, Bedford Indiana. Stephanie N. Vines, Site Manager, Washington County Historical Society, Depot Railroad Museum, Salem Indiana. Stephanie also introduced me to the Monon Railroad Historical-Technical Society. And Tonya Chastain, Lawrence County Tourism Executive Director, Limestone Country, Mitchell Indiana. Thank you all.

About the Author

Dan Sanders is the storyteller of the Tales of Two Counties. He's enjoyed traveling south, spinning yarns, and listening to other folks' fabulous fables for years. Now he's publishing his rip-roaring, hair-raising, rapid-fire reports, starting with *Screams of Late Spring: A Rebel Joe Story*. While not writing, Dan is an accomplished technologist in the data sciences. He is also an avid space launch and exploration enthusiast. Dan lives in Carmel, Indiana, with his wife Becky and near his two grown children, Luke and Emily. They enjoy taking long walks along the West Fork and the Old Monon Railroad trail. And Dan enjoys trading tales with his readers.

Please reach out and say, "Hey!"

Web: http://www.DanSandersSays.com

Email: author@dansanderssays.com

CPSIA information can be obtained
at www.ICGtesting.com
Printed in the USA
LVHW041539260121
677549LV00019B/3349

9 781735 239538